THE TRUTH CHRONICLES

BOOK 3: THE RESCUE

TIM CHAFFEY & JOE WESTBROOK

ILLUSTRATED BY
MELISSA "INKHANA" MATHIS

Risen Books
Richmond, Kentucky

2019

The Truth Chronicles: The Rescue
Copyright © 2010 by Tim Chaffey & Joe Westbrook.
All rights reserved.
Second Printing, 2019

Edited by Reagen Reed
Illustrated by Melissa "Inkhana" Mathis

www.RisenBooks.com
Risen Books is an imprint of Risen Ministries, LLC
Richmond, Kentucky

ISBN-13: 978-0-9840931-4-4
ISBN-10: 0-9840931-4-1

Printed in the United States of America

For Kayla and Judah

PROLOGUE

D r. Thompson," said a voice with a thick Spanish accent.

The doctor spun around to see a huge, muscle-bound man entering the room. "This is Juan. He's the engineer you requested." He nudged the smaller man next to him. "We'll be expecting results very soon."

Dr. Thompson looked Juan over. "I asked for three physical engineers. I need more help."

Glaring, the man crossed his arms and rested them on his puffed-out chest. "Perhaps I was unclear. This is your help." He turned and left the room.

Great. I'll never finish this. With a cursory glance at Juan, Dr. Thompson turned back to his work.

"Dr. Thompson," Juan said as he held out his hand. It trembled as he turned it over to reveal a tiny object in his palm. "They wanted me to give you this microchip."

Taking the chip, Dr. Thompson muttered, "Thanks."

"How long have you been working on this?" Juan asked.

Dr. Thompson spun and faced him. "Why do you care? You work for the group that kidnapped me."

Juan looked stunned. "I don't think you understand. I'm a prisoner. Like you."

Even through his anger, Dr. Thompson saw the pain in Juan's eyes. "I'm sorry. I didn't know. Do... do you have any family?"

Juan's eyes welled up with tears, and he looked down. "I hope so. I was asleep in my home when they broke in. The last thing I remember was hearing my wife scream. When I woke up this morning, I was here."

"Do you happen to know where 'here' is?"

Juan shook his head. "No, I'm sorry." After a few moments of silence, he asked, "Have you thought about escaping?"

Dr. Thompson sympathized with Juan's story but still didn't trust him. "Of course I've thought about it. Every day for the past three years." He sighed. "But it's not an option. They'd kill my family if I tried anything."

"Three years." Juan said as he we wiped his eyes. "But if your family is still alive, then maybe mine is too. I guess we'd better do what they want." After a few quiet moments, he leaned in close. "So there's really no way out of here?"

Dr. Thompson's suspicion grew and he set the microchip down. "No. There's no way out."

"That will be enough talk about escape, gentlemen." The familiar voice of his captor came through the speaker on the wall. "The only way

6

you will ever be freed is if you give us what we want. Now get to work."

We'll see about that. Dr. Thompson looked at Juan, who slumped his shoulders and buried his face in his hands. "I'll give you a few minutes before I explain what we're doing."

Juan sat down in a nearby chair. "Thank you."

Dr. Thompson walked over to a cluttered work-table. He picked up a small transmitter he had been working on and slid a battery into it. Please let this work.

He knew he was taking a risk since he was under constant surveillance, but he had to take the chance. He pushed the small button that would cause the transmitter to send out a signal carrying his old access codes from the Bureau. A small red light blinked for a few seconds before Dr. Thompson pulled the battery and disassembled the device.

ONE

Jax yelled, but the raging current that had pulled him over the top of the waterfall quickly choked out the sound. Time seemed to slow as he fell. He tried to locate JT, who still clung to his hand, but the cascading water made it impossible to see clearly. *Why are we still falling?*

Jax tightened his grip on JT, shut his eyes, and braced for impact.

WHAM! Jax slammed into the turbulence, and every nerve in his body screamed in pain. Everything went black as he twisted and turned under the enormous force pulling him deeper. As he gained a measure of stability, he realized JT was gone. Direction was impossible to determine. Jax paddled and kicked for all he was worth in an effort to get himself free of the turmoil.

A few moments later the water was less chaotic, but the surface was nowhere in sight. His lungs burned, and he continued swimming until his hands hit something hard. *The bottom!* Jax fought the urge to panic. *Think. Get your feet under you. Push!*

A few seconds later, his head broke the surface of the water, and he gasped for air. He half-floated, half-swam toward the nearest bank, all the while looking around for JT. *Where is she? Please, God, help me find her.*

The river grew shallow quickly as he neared the bank, and it wasn't long before he could touch the bottom. He planted his feet and turned around, frantically scanning the river.

"JT! JT!" *C'mon, where are you?* "JT!"

All of a sudden, he saw her arms flailing above the rapids about fifteen feet downstream and closer to the opposite bank. She's alive! Gathering all the strength he had left, he surged back into the river.

He moved quickly as he swam with the current, but when she went under he wasn't sure if he could make it in time. *Hang in there, JT. Just a few more seconds.* Kicking furiously, churning through the water, he managed to reach her just as she went down again. He put his arm under both of her arms and pulled back. "I gotcha. I won't let you go. We're gonna make it." He angled for the nearest shore, allowing the current to do most of the work.

Once he was able to touch bottom again, he stood and used both arms to drag JT along while she coughed and gagged repeatedly. After reaching the shore, he gingerly laid her down on some soft grass.

His arms and legs felt like lead as he fell back against the ground, breathing hard. Jax slowly sat up and noticed that JT had rolled to her stomach and continued to cough and spit up water. He gently placed his hand on her shoulder as she tried to catch her breath.

"Are you okay?" he asked.

She took a couple of deep breaths then turned slowly to look up at him. "Yeah…thanks to you."

"We need to get going," Jax said. "We've got to find a way back up." He extended a hand to JT.

She took it and tried to stand. Her knees buckled once, but she caught herself before falling. She gained her balance and said, "Thanks again."

He smiled and then looked up to the top of the falls to search for his friends. "Izzy! Mick—"

"No," JT said, grabbing his arm. "We're on the same side of the river as Al now."

"Oh, I didn't even think about that." He scanned the canyon wall behind them. It was thickly forested and very steep. "Let's follow the river and see if we can find a place to cross. Then we can worry about finding a way up."

They walked alongside the river, moving west, away from the waterfall, with clothes and hair dripping. Jax listened carefully for any sign of the allosaurus, but only heard the crashing water and their shoes squeaking.

After several minutes the thunder of the falls quieted. JT rolled her sleeves up past her elbows. "You know, Jesus said that the greatest love a person could show to someone else is if they lay down their life for a friend. He did that for us and showed how much He loved us, and you just showed that you're willing to do the same."

been farther apart genetically than Micky and me or you and Izzy."

Jax thought for a few moments about some of his biology lessons on genetics. He soon arrived at the conclusion that what she said made sense. "That is cool. I never thought about it before. You know, that makes a lot more sense than what we were taught. Evolutionists have a problem with everyone coming from two perfect people but will believe that everyone came from one cell."

"Yeah, it takes a lot more faith to believe that it all happened by chance than it does to believe that God made everything."

"You said that Eve was the mother of all the living. Well, if that's true, then that would mean that we are all related, right?"

"Right."

Jax shrugged his shoulders. "Then where did the different races come from? I mean, Izzy is African American. Micky's mom is from India and her dad is Caucasian. But you're saying that we're all related."

JT nodded. "Yeah, if we all come from Adam and Eve, then we would have to be. Besides, like we just talked about, even the evolutionists say that we all go back to a common ancestor, so it's pretty hypocritical if they attack the Bible on this point."

"But it's still a fair question."

"It is, and the Bible gives us the answer. It says—"

Suddenly a high-pitched whistle echoed through the trees on the other side of the river.

"What was that?" she asked, stopping in her tracks.

Jax stared in the direction of the noise and heard branches snapping and leaves rustling. "I don't know, but we'd better get out of sight. Come on."

Izzy pressed himself flat against the ground as his brain registered the scene before him. Darting here and there among terrified villagers, men on horses threw burning torches onto straw roofs. Other horses plunged through the billowing smoke of huts already burning, their riders striking right and left as hapless men, women, and even children came within reach. Izzy gasped and turned his head away.

Micky slowly crawled up the hill to his side. "What did you see?"

He tried to gather his breath and his thoughts before whispering, "There are *people* down there."

Micky started to climb to her feet. "I wanna see."

"No." Izzy grabbed her shoulder and pulled her back down. "It's not just people. There's a small village that's burning to the ground. It's under attack. I saw... I saw—"

"What? What is it?"

15

He slowly shook his head. "People are dying."

"What? Izzy, there can't be people down there. We just saw dinosaurs a couple hours ago."

He rolled onto his back and pressed his hands to his head. "I know. I know. *Was it just an illusion?* He looked at Micky. "Maybe my eyes were just playing tricks on me."

"I'll check it out," she said as she crawled toward the top of the hill.

Taking a deep breath, Izzy rolled over and crept after her, barely noticing the sting of the thistle that stabbed his elbow. He kept his head low as he followed her to the top of the hill and gazed through the long grass.

Below, the small village still burned while a few people fled to the south. A man on horseback held his sword high and yelled. A group of armed men on horses soon gathered around him. With a great shout, they charged after those who had escaped.

"Why would they do that?" Micky asked. Her voice was no more than a whisper.

"I don't know. It's awful. Those poor people." The smell of smoke permeated the air as the wind shifted. Izzy swallowed hard, staring out at the burning huts below. "There shouldn't even be people here. It doesn't make any sense."

"I don't know, but I hope it's not much more, because these trees and the canyon walls are starting to block out the sun. I just hope our clothes finish drying before it cools down."

"It's like we're in a war movie." From the corner of his eye, Izzy saw the color drain from Micky's face as she looked too long at one of the still forms scattered among the ruined huts.

"Yeah, only a hundred times worse. I think I'm gonna be sick." She stopped and cocked her head. "What was that?"

Ahead, movement caught Izzy's eye. "Look." He ran toward a young boy lying on the ground in the middle of the charred village's main road. "He's moving."

When he arrived at the injured boy, the kid's eyes widened and he recoiled, grunting in pain. Izzy slowly knelt and placed his hand on the boy's head. "It's alright, I'm here to help."

Sliding his backpack off, he assessed the boy's condition, swiftly noting the two serious injuries among the myriad scrapes and bruises. "Hurry up, Micky. He's bleeding."

She hustled over. "How bad is it?"

"I need you to squeeze the pressure point in his upper arm and keep it elevated." He looked up, and she nodded. "I'm going to use a makeshift tourniquet to see if we can get this thing stopped."

Micky followed his instructions. As she held the boy's arm she said, "Just stay calm. You're gonna be okay."

The boy looked at Micky and spoke a couple of incomprehensible words.

Izzy dug into his backpack, pulled out a shirt, and tore a couple of strips from it. He quickly wrapped the boy's upper left arm and tied an overhand knot. "See if you can find a stick that we can use to tighten this." Izzy let go of the knot and took Micky's place in applying pressure on the boy's arm.

"I see one," Micky said as she stood. She vanished momentarily and then reappeared holding a stick. "Here you go."

Izzy placed it on top of the knot, and then made another overhand knot. The boy cried as Izzy slowly twisted the stick to tighten the tourniquet. Before long, the bleeding from the boy's arm slowed, and Izzy quickly dressed the wound. "Now, let's take a look at that leg."

Micky knelt and tried to calm the boy by gently rubbing his head. "That one doesn't look too bad."

Izzy pulled the animal hide clothing away from the wound. "Yeah, I think I can take care of that with a couple of bandages. Hand me my backpack."

As he finished bandaging the boy's leg, a cry pierced the air. His eyes met Micky's. "What was that?"

"It sounded like a baby." She was on her feet before he could stop her. "I'll be right back."

"Be careful."

Izzy slowly loosened the tourniquet and checked to see if the bleeding had stopped. Then he grabbed a water bottle from his backpack and helped the boy take a few sips.

"Look what I found," Micky said.

He looked up to see her standing next to him with a baby in her arms. His stomach tightened, and the bottle fell from his hands. *What are we doing?* "Micky, we can't be doing this."

"What do you mean?"

"We're saving the lives of two people in the past that probably would have died. Do you realize what kind of impact this could have on our world?"

Micky staggered back a couple of steps. She looked down at the helpless child in her arms. "What do you want us to do? We can't just put things back the way they were."

Izzy thought before answering. Micky was right. There was no way either of them was going to harm the children they had just rescued. "I'm not sure. I…I think we should just leave the baby with him."

"Why don't we just take them with us?" Micky paused. "No, that wouldn't work either." She paced with the baby in her arms then stopped and pointed. "I think somebody's coming."

Izzy jumped to his feet. Far in the distance, through the smoke, a woman ran toward them. She was dressed in clothes similar to those worn by the boy at their feet. "She looks like someone from this village. Let's just leave the baby here with this boy. We'll watch from a distance to make sure everything goes okay."

Micky kissed the baby on the forehead and gently set her down next to the boy, who viewed them both with wide brown eyes. "Alright, come on."

From the safety of the hill, Izzy and Micky watched the woman run into the town. She wailed as she looked around frantically and then raced over to the young boy and picked up the baby.

"I think she's going to take care of them," Micky said.

"I think you're right. Let's go. We need to find out what happened to Jax and JT."

They walked around the backside of the hill, trying to keep out of sight. "Let's find a way down to the river," Micky said. "Maybe there's a path that the people from this town would take."

She was right. They soon found some steps carved into the steep cliff that led to the river.

Izzy paused and looked back to the village. *I can't believe we were so careless.* He shrugged and started down the stairs.

"Izzy, how do you explain that we just saw people living at the time of the dinosaurs?" Micky asked as they made their way down the steep stairs carved into the face of the cliff. "You know I don't buy JT's Bible stories about that, but I can't deny what I've seen today."

"I don't know. I've been thinking about that too. I can only think of two possibilities. First, JT's right, which would mean the Bible is right." Izzy hesitated and looked at the river valley below as he thought about what those words might mean to his own worldview.

"Or..." Micky asked, making it clear that she wasn't pleased with that option.

"Oh... Or, um, maybe we really are only forty-five hundred years in the past and somehow this place has remained fairly isolated from the rest of the world for the past sixty-five million years. So when the rest of the dinosaurs went extinct, these ones somehow survived. Millions of years later, people evolved, found this area and have been living with them ever since."

Micky jumped over the last few steps and landed on the ground. "There's got to be another solution. That just seems way too far-fetched. I mean, Occam's Razor says that you go with the simplest explanation. If I had to pick between those two, I would say the biblical view is more likely, but I can't accept that."

They walked in the direction of the waterfall. A soft breeze cooled Izzy's face. He considered

Micky's words carefully and knew she was right. "Yeah, that one is pretty ludicrous, which, like you said, would leave us with the biblical view. So, if that is the best solution, why would you say that you can't accept it?"

"Come on, Izzy. Do you really think that there's just one religion that has a corner on the truth? There are so many other religions out there and millions of people that sincerely follow them. If the Bible is right, then they are all wrong. I just don't buy that."

"But you wouldn't do the same thing in science, would you?"

"What do you mean?"

"I mean, what if all the evidence pointed to a conclusion that you didn't like and none of the alternatives made any sense? Would you still reject it?"

"No, I would go along with it. But…but what if we really are seventy million years in the past… and…and the people we saw came here from the future? If you guys invented a time machine, then maybe somebody else could have done it, too."

Izzy contemplated Micky's new proposal, but quickly realized some of the problems with it. "That's impossible."

"Why? What's so impossible about it?"

"Well, it's not impossible to think that someone else may have time-traveled back here. But you've got bigger problems. For example, the locations of the stars provide powerful evidence that we're only thousands of years in the past—not millions. You saw the planetarium show. There's no way to get past that. Plus, what about the fruit trees and the horses those attackers were riding on? Did the alleged people from the future bring those back in the time machine, too?"

"They could have."

"But Micky, you're right back to the problem of Occam's Razor. Your proposal is outlandish compared to what JT says. Think about it. If she's right about the existence of God, then her view makes more sense."

"That's a big 'if,' Izzy."

"I'm not saying I believe it. You know I don't. But our predictions about this place have failed so far, while she's been right on several counts."

Micky sighed and crossed her arms. "Well, I just don't get her."

"Who? JT?"

"Yeah. You know, she follows a religion that is so intolerant, by her own admission, but she's probably the sweetest and most honest person I know. Explain that to me."

"You're right. I can't think of anyone that I would trust more than her." He searched for an explanation. "Maybe she actually just practices what she preaches. After all, didn't Jesus say that we're supposed to love other people?"

"I don't know. I've never read the Bible, so I really wouldn't know what He said."

"That's strange," Izzy said.

"What is?"

"That you are so strongly opposed to JT's view, but you haven't really even studied it."

"Look, Christianity might work fine for her, but it's not for everyone. Besides, even if there is a God, why would there only be one way to get to Him?" She quickened her pace. "Let's just focus on finding them."

They walked in silence for several minutes before Micky asked, "What if they didn't make it?"

Izzy stopped and looked at her. Her arms were folded tight, and she stared at the ground. He tried to think of some comforting words, but his own worries about his friends' safety occupied his mind.

"I don't think I could handle it if they...if they are..." She hesitated for a few moments before finishing. "If they didn't make it."

"Don't even talk like that. They'll be fine," he said, trying to maintain a steady confidence in his voice. "You'll see."

"I sure hope you're right."

"Me too."

Izzy tried to push away the horrible thought of losing two of his best friends, but the tight fear in his stomach wouldn't go away. Trying to focus on something else, he stared at the vegetation to his right. *Under different circumstances, this place would be amazing. What if—*

Micky grabbed his arm. "Did you hear that?"

Izzy said nothing, every sense on edge as he scanned the river bank in front of him.

"Izzy! Micky! Over here!"

Izzy turned his head to his left and noticed Jax and JT standing on the other side of the river and waving their arms in the air. Relief flooded his heart, but before he could respond Micky hugged him tight.

"They made it," she said.

"I told you they would," he said as she released him. "But I was worried too."

Izzy walked toward the water's edge and yelled, "Are you guys okay?"

"Yeah, we're a little wet, but we're fine," Jax yelled back. "How did you guys get down here?"

Izzy pointed. "There's a stairway carved into the side of the cliff back there." He studied the river and determined it was about fifty feet wide and the current was mild. "Do you think you can swim across?"

Jax and JT had a brief conversation before Jax looked up. "Hold on. We're on our way."

Jax walked toward the edge of the river with JT following closely behind him. Suddenly, Micky screamed in terror.

THREE

Without warning, the water erupted to Izzy's left. "Look out!" He yanked Micky away from the river and the giant mouth that had just emerged from it. In a heartbeat, jaws full of massive teeth clamped down, missing Micky's arm by a few inches.

They ran away from the river and looked back at the front half of an enormous crocodile. The creature did not chase them, but instead opened its jaws wide and waited quietly. Micky turned to Izzy and tried to catch her breath. "Look at the size of that thing!"

Izzy remained silent as he stared at the crocodile, which must have been at least thirty feet long. After a few moments, he looked over at Jax and JT, who had backed away from the shore.

"Forget it! I'm not swimming across this river with that thing in it," JT yelled.

Jax cupped his hands to his mouth. "Izzy, we'll have to find another way up. There's no way we're crossing here."

Izzy nodded in agreement as he shouted back, "See if you can make it back to the top of the falls. We'll go back to the car and hover across to get you." Izzy suddenly remembered the phone in his pocket. "Hey Jax, do you have your phone?"

Jax quickly searched his pockets and found

his phone. He played with it for a few seconds. Then he looked at JT, and she shook her head. "I think mine died when we were in the water. JT's is in the car."

Izzy was about to ask Micky if she had her phone when she said, "Mine's in the car too."

"Hey, Jax, catch." Izzy whipped his phone through the air over the gently flowing water. Jax took several steps to the side and back as he reached both hands up to catch it.

"What do you want me to do with it?"

"When we get back to the car, we'll use the walkie-talkie feature on Micky's to keep in touch with you. Just turn it off for the next hour or so to save the battery. We'll call you when we get there."

"Good idea," Jax said as he slid the phone into his pocket. "We're going to keep walking downstream to see if there's a way out of this valley."

"There's no end in sight," Jax said as he scanned the canyon wall stretching upward behind the woods to their right. "It seems like we'll never get out."

JT grabbed his arm and pulled him to a stop. "Do you have any rope in that backpack?"

"Yeah, I packed a bunch of survival gear in here. Why?"

"We could try to scale that wall."

He looked at where she was pointing. "Are you

serious? I don't think I could ever make it up that thing. It's got to be almost a hundred feet high."

"Well, you might not be able to make it, but I'm pretty sure I can."

He put his hands on his hips. "And what makes you think you can do all that?"

"There's a climbing wall at the camp I go to every summer. It's sixty feet high, and I can usually make it without any problems."

"Yeah, but I'm sure you're also tied to something so that it's safe. There's nothing here to help you out."

She held her hands up. "I don't know if we have any other options. It's getting late, and I certainly don't want to be walking out here in the dark. There's no way that I'm going in the water again, so we might as well give it a shot."

Jax wanted to object. He wasn't wild about the prospect of seeing JT clinging to tenuous hand holds eighty feet off the ground. Nor was he wild about the idea that JT could do an athletic feat he couldn't. *What other choice do we have?* "I guess we could at least walk through the woods to see what the cliff wall looks like."

As they walked into the woods, JT said, "Look at the bright side. At least we won't run into any more of those crocodiles."

He smiled, but her comment made him wonder what other dangers might be lurking in the woods.

When they reached the base of the wall, Jax looked up and immediately shook his head. "This is too dangerous. There's no way you can make it up that. Besides, even if you do get up, what happens to me? I can't make it."

"So what? At least I'll be safe." JT winked.

Jax smiled and then turned serious as he watched her study the wall. "That has to be higher than your rock wall at camp."

"Yeah, but not much. Plus, it's not a sheer face, and look at all the small trees jutting out. I can use those for supports." She continued to examine the wall for a few more seconds, then looked him in the eyes. "It doesn't look too bad."

Jax took a step back and shook his head. "Are you serious?"

"Of course. How long is that rope?"

"I don't know," he said as he slid his damp backpack down his arm and dropped it onto the ground. He pulled out the rope and measured it off using his arm as a yard stick, "Looks like about thirty feet."

She glanced back up the cliff. "Alright, here's the deal. I'll tie the rope around my waist and then climb up to that tree about twenty feet up. Once I get there, I'll tie one end of the rope around the tree and drop the other end down to you. Then you can walk up the wall—kinda the opposite of rappelling."

"So how badly do you think we messed things up?" Micky asked, pushing aside a whip-like branch and ducking under another as she and Izzy trekked through the woods on their way back to the time machine. In the distance to their right, smoke from the still-smoldering village shrouded the sky in a gray haze.

"You mean by saving that kid?"

"Yeah."

Izzy rubbed his forehead. "I'm not sure. Maybe not at all. What if that woman would have been able to save him? If that's the case, then he'll just have some memories of some strangers helping him out."

"But that could change his life, too, which could then impact someone else's life and so on."

"I know. We never should have interfered. My guess is that we didn't change things too much. After all, we're still alive, and so are Jax and JT. If we changed something that would ultimately affect us, I think it would've had an immediate impact."

Micky paused, yanking the band from her ponytail and shaking a few leaves out of her hair before pulling it up again. "You mean if that kid grows up to marry one of my ancestors who would have married someone else instead, then I would have never been born. So you think I would have just disappeared immediately?"

"It sounds weird, but, yeah, I think that's what would happen."

Micky grinned as they started walking again. "Then you'd probably be gone too."

"Why? I doubt that we're that closely related."

"Because if I didn't exist, then you wouldn't have gotten out of that tree. After all, I helped build the hover devices."

Izzy thought a moment about what she said. "You're right. Sort of makes you think about how every decision you make could have huge consequences, huh?"

"That's what I was thinking."

FOUR

"Okay, make a loop with the rope and sit in it. You can use it as a seat when you start climbing up. I'll try to take up the slack as you climb," JT said as she looked down at Jax.

He followed her directions and took a deep breath. *Here goes nothing.* He reached up, grabbed the first handhold and slowly started his ascent. "You know, this isn't as hard as I thought it would be."

JT grunted. "That's because I'm pulling some of your weight."

After a minute or so of slow but steady progress, he had nearly reached her perch. "Just a little more," she said as he took his left hand off the rope and grabbed one of the small branches of the tree. He double-checked his footing, and with one last push, he joined her on the tiny outcropping.

"Whew," he said, wiping the sweat off his forehead with the back of his hand. "I think we might just pull this off."

He unfastened the rope from around his waist as she untied the other end from the tree trunk. She surveyed the wall for their next goal. "It looks like we'll have to go sideways a little bit to reach the next tree."

Jax looked at the path they needed to take and noticed there weren't as many places to grip. "Are you sure you can make it there?"

"I'll be fine. Actually..." she paused as she leaned over toward the tree trunk again and wrapped the rope back around it. She made a knot and then tied the other end around her own midsection. "At least I won't fall all the way if I slip." She must have noticed his concern because she immediately said, "Don't worry. I'll be fine."

"You'd better be. Here, I'll give you a boost." He clasped his hands together and held them low enough for her to use as a step.

She studied the wall for a few seconds before reaching up with her left hand and placing her right foot in his hands. "Here we go."

She climbed about ten feet up before she paused and looked to her right. "I think I'm going to move right here, then I'll climb up to the next tree."

"Okay, just be careful."

Once she was safely resting on the tree, Jax untied the rope from the trunk on which he was resting and looped it into a makeshift harness. "Make sure that thing is secure, because I need to swing over before I can start climbing."

She double-checked the rope. "It'll hold."

He made sure the rope was taut then slid out to his right. When he stopped swinging, he planted his feet and started climbing. Soon he had reached the second tree.

"Looks like we're about halfway," he said as he tried to catch his breath. "Are you still doing alright?"

JT nodded and said, "Yep. Better than you. Maybe you should lay off of those Gigabyte burgers."

He laughed and patted his stomach. "Yeah, let's take a quick break."

Her eyes sparkled as she looked out over the valley. He continued to watch her as she closed her eyes and took a deep breath. "The air here is so fresh."

Jax took in the surroundings. Beyond the tree-tops, the river meandered off into the horizon as the sun's rays danced on the water.

"So are you ready yet?" JT asked.

"As ready as I'll ever be."

Once they reached the next ledge, she said, "It looks like another fifteen feet and we're there."

Jax rolled to his back and tried to catch his breath. "That shouldn't be too bad. To be honest, I didn't think we would make it this far. It's a good thing you know what you're doing."

She smiled. "Well, somebody has to save our skins."

Jax chuckled and rolled to his right side. When he did, he felt the bump of Izzy's phone in his front pocket. "Oh, I forgot all about this." He pulled the phone out and turned it on. "Hey, Izzy, did you guys make it back yet?"

There was no response.

"Well, I guess it will probably take them a while to walk back through the woods."

"Yeah, I hope they're safe. Are you ready to start climbing again?" she asked as she secured the rope around her waist.

"Ladies first," he said with a grin.

Once again, she scaled the wall quickly. When she reached the top, she moved out of sight for a few seconds then peered over the edge and said, "It's all set."

He grabbed a small handhold to begin scaling the wall when a tremendous roar reverberated through the trees. "What was that?" As the last word left his mouth, JT reappeared above him. She grabbed the rope and swung her legs over the edge. She was climbing back down. Fast.

The bottom end of the rope was still tied around him. He fumbled at the knot, but she was coming too quickly. Just in time, he reached up and caught her around the waist before she slammed into him. "Whoa, slow down. Was that what I think it was?"

She spun around and backed up against the side of the cliff. Her pale face and wide eyes told him the answer before she even spoke. "I'm not sure, but I really don't want to find out."

When another roar ripped through the air, Jax quickly untied the rope from his waist and backed up next to her. He heard the advance of thunderous footsteps and the unmistakable sound of branches and twigs crackling under immense weight. He looked at JT and whispered, "Do you think it's Al?"

"I hope not," she mouthed.

The footsteps grew louder and louder, and it seemed as if the cliff itself was trembling. She grabbed his hand and squeezed it hard.

The sensation of her hand in his made him momentarily forget the danger, but a coughing snort from the creature above jolted him back to the present. He looked up and determined that if they moved a few feet to their right, they would be under a small bulge in the wall that would hide them from the view of anything above. Stepping quietly toward the sheltering rock, he tugged on JT's hand to get her to move, but she wouldn't budge.

The footsteps and the creature's heavy breathing filled Jax's eardrums. He tugged JT's hand harder and frantically pointed in the air to get her attention. As a cascade of dirt and small chunks of rock landed in her hair, she blinked and then moved next to him.

There was a sudden stillness broken only by the unmistakable breathing. Jax pressed his back tightly against the wall next to JT and felt it shake when the creature took another step.

Suddenly, the breathing stopped. Jax held his breath and it appeared to him that JT was doing the same. After what seemed like minutes, the creature sniffed the air.

Jax's curiosity got the best of him. He leaned toward JT and peered up and around her. Sticking out over the edge of the cliff was a massive head and neck that looked all too familiar. Just two weeks earlier, he had been lying on a similar rock ledge looking up into the eyes of the same hungry dinosaur.

Without warning, the beast, which had been looking out over the river far below, shifted its head and looked straight down the face of the cliff. Jax jumped back against the wall. He squeezed JT's hand tightly and pulled her close.

God, please don't let that thing see us. The creature snorted and took a step. Jax saw the dangling section of the rope sway. A shriek pierced the air, and Jax thought his heart skipped a beat. He looked up and saw a small flying dinosaur glide over them. Al snorted and then roared.

The footsteps started again, and Jax's stomach felt like it was tied in a knot. The stomping grew quieter, and his fears lessened with each step as he realized the dinosaur was leaving.

Once he was confident the creature was out of range, Jax whispered, "That sure looked like Al."

Color returned to JT's face, and she started taking full breaths again. "How can you tell?"

"I'd know those teeth anywhere." He paused. "I think he likes me."

She gave a half-smile then whispered, "I think

44

he walked away from the falls. We should be able to wait for a while and then make a break for it."

"What if he comes back while we're walking?"

JT released his hand and brushed some debris from her hair. "We'll just keep really quiet and walk along the edge of the cliff. If we hear it getting closer, we'll tie the rope to a tree near the edge and hang from it. Hopefully, there will be another ledge like this time."

He dusted himself off too. "Hopefully, we don't have to find out."

"Right where we left it," Micky said. "Let's hurry up. I'll feel a lot safer once we're inside."

They ran to the car. Izzy took off his backpack, threw it into the backseat and then climbed in, while Micky jumped in the driver's seat for the first time. "We made it," she said with a huge sigh.

Izzy closed his eyes and took a deep breath, momentarily enjoying the relative safety of the car. "Hey, grab your phone and try to get a hold of Jax."

"Oh yeah." She reached back, grabbed her purse, and rifled through it until she found the phone. "Got it." After pushing a few buttons to turn on the walkie-talkie feature, Micky asked, "Hey, Jax, are you out there?" After a long pause, she tried again. "Jax, JT, are you guys there?" There was still no response.

She looked concerned, so Izzy said, "Don't worry yet. I told him to turn it off to save the battery. Just leave it on in case they call. Let's head to the falls. Maybe they will already be there waiting for us."

"Sounds like a plan." She started the car, and Izzy engaged the hover technology.

"Let's cross the river before we get any closer."

"Good thinking."

Izzy grabbed the joystick and guided the car across, then turned the car to follow the river. He kept his head on a swivel and his hands near the controls in case they needed to elevate away from danger at a moment's notice. When they were about fifty feet from the waterfall, he set the car down.

"Nicely done." Micky looked at the gauges in front of her. "It looks like we're at full power, so let's pack up the solar panels."

She popped the trunk, and Izzy got out and put them away. Just then, the phone chirped, and JT's voice came over the speaker.

Twenty minutes had passed since Al left. Jax looked at JT. "Let's get going. We'll have plenty of warning if he comes back." Jax fashioned a harness again from the dangling rope. "I'll go up first this time."

He was determined to make things easier for

her, and with great effort he reached the top. He scanned the area for danger and then dropped one end of the rope down and helped her up.

"Thanks. That was much easier," she said as she untied the rope from her waist.

Jax untied the other end and wound the rope into several loops. He slid the coil into his backpack and slung it over his shoulder. "Let's get moving."

They walked through the forest of towering trees toward the falls. He heard countless animal sounds echoing through the woods and guessed that most were the songs of birds.

"These are the biggest trees I've ever seen," JT said.

"Yeah, they look like the redwoods back home."

"Really? If they are this cool, then I can't wait to see them. We planned to go once, but my little brother got sick so we had to cancel."

"Well, if you take Botany next year, then you'll get to. Mr. Doniger takes his class there every year."

"That's right." She looked up to the treetops and smiled. "I was trying to decide if I should take that class. I think I just made up my mind."

He looked at her and smiled. *And I guess I'll be taking it, too.*

"You know," she said and slowly turned toward him. "We could take a day trip to the redwoods with Izzy and Micky."

"Yeah, that would be—Oh." He reached into

his pocket. "I should try Izzy again." He pulled the phone out and powered it up again.

JT held out her hand. "Here, let me call them."

He gave her the phone and she called.

"Izzy, are you there?" she asked. After a few seconds she said, "Oh hey, Micky, are you guys alright? ...Yeah, we made it up. You should see the trees here. ...I'll tell you about it later. I'd rather not make too much noise right now. I think we should be there in about an hour. ...Okay, I'll buzz you again when we're close. ...Alright, 'bye."

She put the phone in her pocket and looked at him. "They're waiting for us at the top of the falls."

"Good, let's pick up the pace."

They continued moving quickly but quietly through the woods. During their hour-long walk, Jax kept listening for the slightest hint of the allosaurus, especially as the forest grew darker and the animal noises picked up. One particular animal scream caused JT to jolt and put her hand over her heart, but there was no sign of Al.

Relief came over Jax when he heard the familiar crashing sound of the waterfall. "We must be getting close."

JT reached into her pocket and pulled out the phone. "Hey, Micky, are you still there? ...Yeah, we're getting pretty close. I can see part of the waterfall through the trees here. I'm guessing we're about two hundred yards away. ...Alright, we'll see you in a bit." She handed the phone back to him.

It was then that Jax noticed the lack of forest noises. He looked at JT. As if reading his mind, she stopped, tilted her head, and looked at him.

Jax turned around and scanned the area for signs of danger. He didn't see any, but he didn't need to, because then he heard it. It was a sound that brought instant fear to his heart. Over the pounding of the falls, the terrifying roar of the allosaurus reverberated through the forest.

"Run," he said as he grabbed her hand. They raced through the forest. Ferns slapped against their pant legs, and small branches ripped at their arms and faces.

Jax reached into his pocket and fumbled the phone as he pulled it out, but caught it before it hit the ground. "Izzy, start the car! We're being chased, and we need to leave ASAP!" He looked back and saw movement in the trees far behind them. Adrenaline shot through his body as he surged ahead, practically pulling JT along.

"There's the clearing," JT said. "And the car!"

They broke out of the woods. The passenger side was facing them, and Izzy stood near the open doors, shouting, "Hurry up!" The car was only fifty feet away—thirty—ten.

Jax's heart pounded, and he gasped for air as they reached the vehicle. JT jumped into the back seat and Jax followed close behind her. Before he was even completely in the car, Izzy engaged the hover technology.

As Jax slammed the door, the dinosaur broke through the last bit of forest and stampeded toward them.

"I'm in! Let's go!" As soon as the words left his mouth, Izzy pushed the joystick forward and the car sped toward the river's edge. "Must go faster!" Jax yelled.

Al was closing fast. "Hold on," Izzy said and then slid the levels all the way up. The car shot another forty feet in the air and picked up steam.

Jax turned back and saw the allosaurus slow down and stop at the river's edge. It looked up at the car and belted out a tremendous roar.

Jax looked over at JT and sighed deeply. He put his hand on hers. "That was way too close."

"No doubt." Trembling, she took several quick breaths. "Izzy, let's go home."

"Are you sure you don't want to stick around?" Izzy said innocently.

"No way," Jax and JT said in unison.

Izzy laughed. "Now you know how I felt in that tree. So how did you guys get out of that valley?"

"We'll explain later." Jax slumped in his seat as the adrenaline started to wear off. "Let's just get home."

FIVE

H ey, Jax, it's Micky."

"Hey, what's up?" Jax said into the phone.

"I had an idea. Are you gonna be around the next few days?"

"Yeah, I'm not going anywhere."

"Okay. Well, since JT's at camp and Izzy's on vacation, I thought you could help me with a project."

"Sure. What kind of project?"

"I was hoping to build two more repulsors and attach them to one of these snowboards so we could actually make one of our hoverboards."

"Didn't you say that you couldn't get enough power to make them hover?"

"Yeah, but I was hoping we could use one of your prototype batteries."

Jax thought for a moment before responding. "I guess it depends on if I get to ride it first," he said.

"Great! When can we start?"

"Right away, if you want. Did you want to work on it here?"

"Is that alright?"

"Yeah, I'd actually prefer it. I've got all sorts of tools here. Plus, then I won't have to take the power supply away from home."

"Okay. That works for me. I'll be over after lunch."

"Sounds good. See ya." Jax hung up the phone and sat down at the dining room table. *Now to finish that map.*

He opened the cartography program that Izzy installed on the car's laptop. Studying his journal entry about the trip, he inserted the appropriate symbols for the trees and river and labeled the waterfall and various animals.

There. Izzy will have to do the other side of the river. I gotta get something to eat.

As Jax shoved the last bite of his sandwich into his mouth, his mom walked in, removing her gardening gloves and hat.

"So what are your plans for today?" she asked as she washed her hands in the sink.

Jax took a drink and swallowed. "Micky's coming over in a little bit. We're gonna work on some stuff in the garage."

"Oh, good. I'm glad you'll have something to do. You've been moping around the house ever since JT left."

"Yeah, I wish I had signed up when I had the chance, but back then I didn't even want to go."

"Well, there's always next year." She dried her hands and then came over and put a hand on his shoulder. "Jax, I can't tell you how happy I am that you've made God a part of your life."

He put his hand on hers and squeezed it. "Me too, Mom."

Just then the doorbell rang. "I'll get it. It's probably Micky."

"Alright, just don't forget to cut the grass later."

"I won't." He opened the front door and said, "Hey, perfect timing. I just finished my lunch."

With a laugh Micky stepped inside. "I can tell. You still have a milk mustache."

Mildly embarrassed, Jax wiped his upper lip with the back of his hand. "So are you ready to get started?"

"Yeah, you take these." She handed him the two boxes she had been carrying. "I've got to go get the rest of the stuff out of the car."

"There's more? Alright, just go to the garage door. I'll get it opened up."

Jax carried the boxes to the garage and pressed the door opener. Micky was already on her way up the driveway with another load of supplies, including a snowboard. They walked across the garage floor to "the lab," as he liked to call it.

She laughed as she surveyed the room. "You sure like to keep a clean workplace, huh?"

"Hey, this is how I do my best work." He cleared a spot on the work table by pushing some pop cans onto the floor and organizing a few tools. Then he walked around the car, grabbed a stool, and brought it back to the work table. "Alright, let's get to work. What do we need to do?"

She pulled out her schematic drawings and

other notes and consulted them frequently as she described each step in the assembly process.

"How long do you think this will take?" Jax asked.

"Quite a while. It took JT and me several days before we finished the first one. But the last one only took a day."

"And I thought these things looked pretty basic. Not bad for a couple of girls."

"Hey, I resemble that remark," Micky said. "Speaking of JT…"

He fumbled the screwdriver and both the screw and screwdriver tumbled to the ground. "What about her?"

She giggled. "Well, you know, what's going on with you two?"

"Uh, nothing's going on. We're friends."

"Suuure. I know you like her."

He picked up the screwdriver and screw and started working again. "Of course I do, but we're just friends. I asked her out a couple of weeks ago, but she turned me down."

"Because of your views on God, right?

"Well, I'm not sure if that's the only reason, but we definitely talked about it."

"So that's why you pulled that little stunt at youth group, huh?"

He spun and looked at her. "What stunt? What are you talking about?"

She met his gaze and smiled. "You know, acting like you are a Christian now so she'll like you."

Jax was surprised. He set the screwdriver down and stared at it for a few seconds. *I guess I can see why she would think that.* "Do you really think that's what I'm doing?"

"C'mon Jax. I know you don't really believe all that Bible stuff. You've just been playing along so that she'll like you." She picked up a wire stripper and some wires. "And I think it's working."

She thinks it's working? Does JT really like me? Before dwelling on that too much, he shook his head and tried to focus on the issue at hand. "You're wrong, Micky. I'm not just playing along. I really do believe the Bible...and I am a Christian."

"Well, you would say that either way." She winked. "Because I'm JT's friend and you wouldn't want me to ruin things for you."

He held out his hands. "But I'm not lying. That might be hard for you to believe, but I would never do that to JT. We both know how important her faith is to her, and there's no way I would play games with her like that." He took a deep breath and let it out slowly. "Look, I went to youth group that night with all sorts of questions. I didn't believe the Bible because I thought there were a bunch of things that science had proven wrong. But the message that night convinced me that Jesus really did rise from the dead. And if that's true, then the rest of what He taught is true, too."

"Wait. How would that prove everything else that He taught?"

"Don't you remember what Pastor Rich said? If God raised Jesus from the dead, then that means that He approved of what Jesus taught. Otherwise, God would be putting his stamp of approval on a fraud."

"Whatever," she said as she rolled her eyes. "But what about all that stuff about God creating in six days, just thousands of years ago? What about all the facts we've been taught in school that contradict the Bible? Are you telling me that you're rejecting science, too?"

"Micky, you know that's not true. Jonas obviously doesn't reject science, and you know that JT doesn't either. I still have questions that haven't been answered. I don't know if I agree with everything in Genesis, but I'm at least willing to take a look at it. After all, Jesus said it was true."

She crossed her arms. "What do you mean? When did Jesus say that Genesis was true?"

"I don't remember the exact verse, but I was reading it the other day. He said that the creation of Adam and Eve was 'at the beginning.' The only way Adam and Eve could have been 'at the beginning' is if they were made at about the same time as the universe—like the Bible teaches. Otherwise, He didn't know what He was talking about or He was lying."

"I wouldn't want to say that He was lying, but He probably just adopted the wrong thinking of His day."

"But don't you see?" His eyes locked onto hers. "If He is God, like He claimed to be, then He couldn't lie or be wrong about it. He would know exactly what happened."

"But Jax, we know that science has proven Him wrong."

"That's what I thought too, but we've been debating this topic with JT for a few weeks now, and so far all the evidence is lining up on her side."

She looked down and fidgeted with the cordless drill in her hand. "It is not."

"What about you and Izzy seeing people living at the same time as dinosaurs? What about birds, large mammals, and dinosaurs all at the same time? What about the stars?"

Micky hesitated before answering. "Okay, even if a few things lined up with the biblical view, that doesn't overthrow all the other evidence for evolution."

"What other evidence?"

"What about carbon dating? What about the geologic column and all the fossils? How can you explain all the evidence for evolution if you believe the Bible?"

Jax scratched his head. "I don't know. I've got some of the same questions, and maybe there are good answers for those." He smiled. "I'm new at this, you know. A few weeks ago, I didn't think the Bible could handle any of my questions, but now it seems to give the best answers. I'm at least willing to look into it. What about you?"

She sighed. "I don't think so. I just can't see letting an ancient book written by a bunch of Stone Age people rule my life."

"But what if it's true? What if everything the Bible says is accurate? Would you still reject it? I mean, just because it's old doesn't mean it's not true."

"It just doesn't make any sense to claim that one religion is the only right one."

"So are you saying that it's impossible for one religion to be right and the rest of them to be wrong?"

"In theory, I guess it's logically possible. But, in reality, all religions are essentially the same. They all have bits of the truth and they all provide comfort to their followers."

"That's not true. They aren't all the same, and you know it." He stood and started pacing. "Most religions say that you can get to heaven, or paradise, or whatever you wanna call it, just by being a good person. Christianity says that it's not about what you do, but about what God already did for you when Jesus died on the cross." He stopped and looked at her. "That's completely different. Plus, Christianity is the only religion whose founder claimed to be God and then proved it by rising from the dead."

"So are you saying that anyone who isn't a Christian is gonna go to hell when they die? All those sincere followers of other religions will go to hell? Is that what you believe?"

"Look, I know it's not a comfortable subject, but yes, I would say that, because that's what Jesus said. He said He was the only way to God. And logically, if that's true, then the rest of the religions are false."

Micky dropped the drill on the table and pressed her hands to her head. "Ugghhh…I just can't believe how narrow-minded you Christians are."

Jax let his lips form a little smile. "So you think I'm actually a Christian, then?"

"Well, you sure sound like one lately."

"Micky, I'm not the one being narrow-minded."

"What are you talking about?"

"Let me ask you a question. What do you think happens to a person when they die?"

She bit her lip and hesitated. "I would say that I don't know and that we can't know. I don't think there's really anything beyond this life. We probably just get buried and rot in the ground. But I guess if there is a God, and if there's a heaven, then He would let everyone in because He loves everyone."

"Now that sounds narrow-minded."

"How can you say that?"

"Because you don't even give someone an option. According to you, if there is no God, then everyone rots. If there is a God, then everyone goes to heaven. That's narrow-minded. At least with Christianity you have two options—heaven or hell."

"Whatever. I don't want to fight about this anymore." Micky turned and picked up the drill again. "Let's just get back to work."

Micky set the repulsor on the work table. "That's one down, one to go."

Jax looked at the clock. "Whoa, that really did take all day."

"You wanna finish up tomorrow?"

"Sure, and if we finish in time, then you could come to youth group with me."

Micky hesitated, tracing a crack in the floor with her shoe. *Maybe I could get Jax and JT off my back about the whole God thing by acting like I agree with them. That would make them happy, and we wouldn't always argue about it. I guess youth group was pretty cool—and that drummer sure was cute.*

"Are you okay?" he asked.

She looked up. "Yeah, I'm okay. I was just thinking that...that maybe you guys could be right about all this."

Jax looked confused. "About all of what?"

"You know, God and the Bible."

His eyes widened, and his mouth hung open slightly.

Micky smiled inside as she saw how well her ruse had worked. "I didn't say that I agreed with all of it or that I believe in Jesus and all that stuff, but I've learned a lot over the past few weeks." She searched for the right words to make Jax think she was sincere. "I think I'll keep going to youth group."

He smiled. "Well, that's a start. Let me know if there are any questions I can help you with… or, maybe it's better if you ask JT."

Micky flashed a mischievous look. "So we're back to talking about JT again, huh?"

His cheeks reddened a little. "I guess so. My favorite subject," he said with a goofy grin.

"You're such a dork." She stood up and grabbed her purse. "I'll be back in the morning. Don't forget to order that power converter."

SIX

"W elcome to summer school," Mr. Harmon said. "This is Logic and it will be quite different than what most of you are used to. Instead of all the experiments and lab work that you kids like doing, we're going to be doing some heavy-duty thinking."

"Well, I guess you'd better drop the class now, Ted," Micky said as she leaned forward and nudged his shoulder. Several students laughed.

"I was just about to say the same thing to you, Micky," Ted said.

"Dude, that was lame," William said, and there was more laughter.

Mr. Harmon had a half smile on his face when he continued. "As I was about to say, logic is the art and science of reasoning. In a lot of your classes you are taught *what* to think. In Logic, you are going to learn *how* to think, and to think well."

He sat on the corner of his desk. "Most schools won't ever teach this subject, so you should consider yourselves quite privileged. By the end of these eight weeks, you'll be able to recognize valid syllogisms and spot many of the common mistakes people make when debating. It will help you make stronger arguments and reach sound conclusions in your scientific investigations."

Mr. Harmon continued to lecture for the rest

of the hour. When the bell rang, Jax grabbed his books off his desk. "So, JT, how was camp?"

She turned to look at him as she grabbed her own books. "It was fantastic. I wish you could have been there."

"I know," he said. "So what happened?"

"Oh, a lot of the usual stuff. You know, swimming, hiking, waterskiing, and your favorite, rock climbing."

Jax laughed as they left the classroom, following Izzy and Micky. "Good thing you know how to do that, huh?"

"Oh, you'll never guess who was there to lead one of our activities." She reached forward and tapped Micky's shoulder. "Guess who was at camp for a couple of nights."

Micky and Izzy slowed and glanced back. He shrugged his shoulders. Micky looked at JT and asked, "Tyler the drummer?"

"No. Jonas Ellis. He was there for our two-day hike and led devotions at night under the stars. It was really cool."

Micky walked backward for a few steps, grinning slyly. "Did you ask him out for me?"

JT rolled her eyes. "Nope. Sorry. Must have slipped my mind. Seriously though, I need to tell you the best part. He invited us to the Foothills Observatory this Friday night to see the Morris-Faulkner Comet. He said that he would be there all night doing research and we could stay up there overnight, too."

"Are you serious?" Izzy asked. "That would be awesome."

"Yeah, I'm serious. I'm supposed to call him tonight to let him know if you guys are interested. So that's a 'Yes'?"

"Count me in." Micky turned down a different hallway. "I'm parked out here. Anyone need a ride?"

"I do," Izzy said as he followed after her.

"We're gonna walk. Call me later," JT said.

Jax waved. "See ya."

Moments later, Jax opened the school door for JT. "After you."

"Thanks."

Jax followed her and squinted. "Wow, it's really bright out."

"Sure is." She reached into her purse and pulled out her sunglasses. "So Micky said you guys built an actual hoverboard while I was away and that you saw our secret plans. We'd better not catch you building your own repulsors."

"Don't worry. When I sell the plans, I won't tell Izzy or Micky, and you and I can split the profits fifty-fifty."

She gave him a playful nudge with her elbow as they turned onto a magnolia-lined street.

"We're just waiting on the part I ordered, and then we'll get to try it out. Oh, and speaking of

Micky. While we were working, she said that she thought that the Bible might be right and that she would be willing to look into it more."

Her eyes lit up. "Really? That's great. That's an answer to prayer."

"Yeah, she even came to youth group with me the past two weeks. She seemed to like it."

"Well, that's a good start. Let's keep praying for her."

"Definitely. But what should I do if she asks a question that I don't know how to answer?"

"Well, just tell her you don't know and that you'll try to find an answer. Then be sure to look it up and get back to her. That's what I do, and I think it's always best to be open and honest. People can tell if you are trying to bluff your way through."

"That sounds good." Jax stepped onto a curb and started balancing along it. "So you never finished answering my question about how the Bible explains the different races."

"Oh yeah. Where were we?"

He jumped off the curb. "I think you were just getting started. You said that both creationists and evolutionists agree that we have a common ancestor, but that they disagree on several points."

"Right. Um, well, obviously there are huge differences between the two views. The Bible teaches that we are all descendants of Adam and Eve. Well, also of Noah and his wife, too. The evolutionary belief is that we all go back to a group of ape-like ancestors and way beyond that to a single cell. Actually, if you think about it, the evolutionary view is quite racist."

"Racist? How?"

"Because it teaches that some people groups are more closely related to the apes than others. I'm not saying that all evolutionists are racists. I'm sure most of them aren't, but their theory is.

"Besides, I don't like using the term races to refer to people because there's really only one race—humans. That's why I said people groups."

"Alright, so how does the Bible explain the different people groups?"

She adjusted the books in her arms. "Are you still reading your Bible every day?"

"Yeah, I'm already in the middle of Genesis. Last night I was reading about Jacob and Esau."

"So you read about the Tower of Babel in Genesis 11, right?"

"Oh yeah, you mean when God confused the people's languages?"

"Right. The Bible says that after the Flood the people gathered together and started building the tower. They were supposed to spread throughout the world, but they disobeyed God. So God made them speak different languages. Since they couldn't communicate, they couldn't work together, so they went their separate ways."

"Just like God wanted them to do in the first place," he said.

"Yep. Well, think about what would happen if a group of people that were short went off in one direction and didn't have any contact with another group."

"I suppose if they only had the DNA for short people, then you'd have an entire group of people that were short...like the pygmies in Africa."

"Exactly."

"But, that might explain height, but how does that explain the different skin colors? I doubt that God sent people with light skin in one direction and people with dark skin in another."

"No, I don't think He did, either. Most of the people probably had middle brown skin. Then, when they split up, those who were better suited to their new environments were able to survive. For example, if you've got a group that moved near the Equator, where it's hot and sunny for much of the year, the lighter-skinned people probably wouldn't survive as well. They might get skin cancer and be gone within a few generations. This would leave only the darker-skinned people in that area."

"But I thought you said that the people were middle brown. Where do you get white and black then?" Jax asked as they turned onto JT's street.

"Well, you remember basic biology. If you take two middle brown people, who have the genetic variability for light and dark skin, and they have kids, what color of skin will their kids have?"

"You're talking about Punnett Squares. Well, let's see, most of them would be middle brown, but you could have some that are very light and some that are very dark."

"That's right. There are even some cases where a middle brown couple has twins, but one baby is really light and the other is really dark."

Jax raised his eyebrows. "No way. Really?"

"Yeah, my dad showed me one of his old magazines that had pictures of twin girls in England. The parents were middle brown, but one girl was really dark with brown eyes, and the other girl was really light with blue eyes."

"That's cool. Does he still have that magazine?"

"Probably. I'll see if I can find it for you."

"Okay, you explained how you can get a group of short people or a group of dark-skinned people. But how can you get a group of people that are just white?"

She held her hands out. "Well, it's the same principle, really. What if a group of people split off from Babel and went up to Europe? Many creationists believe there would have been an ice age going on for several hundred years after the Flood."

"Wait a minute. What's this about an ice age?"

"Well, a worldwide Flood, like the one described in Genesis, is the only thing we know of that could start an ice age. But we can talk about that later. Let's get back to the people groups."

"Okay, but we definitely have to talk about this ice age sometime."

"Sure..." she paused and looked up. "Alright, if Europe was in the middle of an ice age and a group of people moved there, who would be more likely to survive?"

Jax thought for a moment. "I suppose the lighter-skinned people, because they don't need as much sunlight for vitamin-D synthesis."

JT smiled. "Wow, vitamin-D synthesis. Those are big words for you. I'm surprised you remember studying that."

Jax grinned. "Hey, I'm not as dumb as I look."

They both laughed and turned up her walkway before she said, "Well, you're right, though. The lighter-skinned people would survive better. After several generations, only light-skinned people would live in that area and they would be the ones having kids. Those with darker skin would be at a much higher risk of heart disease and other problems associated with a lack of vitamin D. So eventually, you would just have lighter people in colder climates and darker people in hot climates. Up until the last couple hundred years, when people started mixing together much more than they had been, that's what we observed in the world."

Jax shook his head.

"What's the matter?'

"I just wish they would teach us this in school. It makes so much more sense."

"I do too." She turned and headed for the front door. "Do you wanna walk to school tomorrow?"

"Sure. I'll be here at eight."

SEVEN

"Wait a minute. This isn't your regular spot. Are you trying to confuse me?" the waitress asked as she flipped to an open page in her order pad.

"We're waiting for someone else to join us," Jax said.

"Okay, darlin', I'll stop back when your friend arrives."

"Thanks."

"This is exciting. I can't wait to see a comet through the telescopes they have up there," Izzy said, practically bouncing on the seat.

"Yeah, I bet everyone in our class would be jealous that we get to spend the whole night at the observatory," Jax said.

"And we'll have Jonas teaching us," Micky said as she winked at JT.

"Speaking of Mr. Ellis, there he is." JT waved her hand to get his attention.

A few seconds later, Jonas stood by their table. "Mind if I join you?"

Micky scooted closer to JT and motioned to the empty spot next to her. "Hi, Jonas. Have a seat."

He sat down and said, "It's good to see you guys again. Are you all set for a full night at the observatory?"

"Almost," Jax said. "We need to head back to

my place to drop off my mom's car. She needs it to go visit a friend tonight. We'll take *the* car."

Izzy cleared his throat. "Um, Jax. Aren't you concerned about driving it around in broad daylight?"

Jonas raised an eyebrow. "Is that the car you told me about?"

"Yeah, I thought you might want to see it." Jax turned to Izzy. "I'm not too concerned. I detached the cable from the front and stuck it in the trunk. That only took a minute, and now it looks pretty much like a normal car."

"A normal, piece of junk car," Micky said.

There were a few chuckles around the table at her comment, but Jax ignored it. "My place is sort of on the way to the observatory, so it won't take long."

"Okay, that works for me," Jonas said. "I would have been willing to go a long way to see it."

The waitress returned and took their orders. "I'll get those right out."

"So have you guys used 'the car' again since the last time I talked to you?" Jonas asked, making quotation marks with his fingers.

Jax looked around and saw that people at the nearby tables seemed to be minding their own business. "Yeah, we decided to go back to the same time period and do some exploring. You wouldn't believe what we saw."

For the next ten minutes, Jax and his friends

filled him in on the details of their excursion. They told him about the ceratopsian herd, the waterfall incident, and their ensuing journeys to find each other and get back to the vehicle. When Izzy and Micky filled him in on the details about the attack they had witnessed and how they helped the young boy and baby, Jonas choked on his water.

"Whoa, wait," Jonas said. "You interacted with people?"

"Yeah," Izzy said. "But it doesn't seem to have impacted anything here."

Jonas rubbed his chin with his finger, his expression thoughtful. "You guys said you went back forty-five hundred years, right?"

"Well, that's what Jax and JT think," Micky said. "But that's debatable."

"Well, I think that makes sense," Jonas said.

"What do you mean?" JT asked.

"The timing. According to the Bible, you guys went back to a time period just before the Flood. The Bible says that men were extremely wicked at that time." He looked at Izzy. "You and Micky certainly witnessed that when you saw the attack on that village. But it also makes sense that your actions didn't impact our world—at least as far as we know. If you guys were interacting with people who lived a short time before the Flood, then these were people that were going to die soon anyway—unless it was Noah's family."

Izzy leaned forward and spoke quietly. "Are you saying that our actions in that time period would probably never impact our world, unless we happened to interfere with Noah and his family?"

"Sure. Why would it? It might affect those people that you interacted with, but unless they had some contact, directly or indirectly, with Noah and his family, then I don't see how it would have any impact on our time."

"So that would mean we could keep going back there and not have to worry about wrecking the present," JT said.

"If you truly are going to that time period, you probably could," Jonas said. "You should still be careful, though."

"If that's true..." Micky started as though she were deep in thought, but then her tone turned playful. "Then all we really have to worry about are dinosaurs, waterfalls, and murderous hordes of people."

Their laughter was interrupted by a loud, "Dude!" Jax looked up and noticed Ted and William coming straight for the table.

"They still let you guys in here?" Micky asked. "I'm gonna have to speak to management."

"Chill, babe," William said. Then he looked at Jonas and paused as if he were thinking deeply—an image he did not put forth often. "I know you. You're that über-smart dude in the trophy case at school. Ellis, right?"

"That's right. And you are?"

"Oh, sorry. I'm Ted." He shook Jonas' hand. "And this is William."

Jonas smiled and said, "It's nice to meet you guys."

"Whoa, it's like meeting a living legend," William said as he ran his fingers through his blond hair. "What are you doing with a bunch of losers like these guys? You should come eat with us."

"Hey, William, who won the science fair?"

"Be quiet, Micky. You chicks were just lucky. We would have won if we didn't get in trouble."

"I guess that makes us winners," she said as she formed a W with her two thumbs and index fingers. "And that would make you two the losers." She formed a backward L with her fingers.

"Whatever. Seriously though, how do you guys know each other?"

"He spoke at our church last year, and my youth pastor put us in touch," JT said.

"Cool," William said and then turned to Ted. "Dude, I'm famished. Let's order something." The two boys said their good-byes and walked to an open booth on the other side of the restaurant.

Before long the waitress brought out their orders. "There you go," she said with a smile. "Can I get you anything else?"

"Not right now," Jax said, glancing at the others. "Thank you."

As she walked away, Jonas looked at the enormous hamburger on Jax's plate. "Now I know what took 'em so long to make our food."

"This is the famous Gigabyte combo—one pound of Angus beef on a toasted bun and loaded with toppings, complete with fries and a drink."

Micky pushed her fork into her salad and was in the middle of raising the first bite to her mouth when Jonas asked, "You want me to pray?"

Micky blushed and set the fork down on the plate. "Oh, sorry. Go ahead."

After Jonas prayed, they made small talk while eating their meals. There was plenty of laughter, especially when Izzy dumped most of the salt container on his fries because Jax had secretly loosened the lid.

"So," Izzy said during one of the few quiet moments when the others had their mouths full. "I've got a question. We've talked a lot about the biblical and evolutionary views over the past month. We've tried to make sense of what we witnessed in the past, and I have to admit, the Bible seems to do a better job of explaining what we've seen." He looked at JT, whose eyebrows had shot up. "But how can a Christian explain dinosaurs? They aren't mentioned in the Bible, right?"

Everyone perked up, and Jax leaned as far forward as possible in anticipation of what Jonas might say.

"That's a great question, Izzy," Jonas said. "In one sense you're right, the word *dinosaur* doesn't appear in the Bible, but there's a good reason for that. *Dinosaur* is a relatively modern word. It wasn't coined until 1841. Yet the first English Bibles were translated hundreds of years before that. So, of course, they wouldn't have used it."

"Okay, I can see that. But it doesn't even mention them by any name, right?"

"Actually, I think it does, but it uses different terminology."

"Do you think the behemoth in Job 40 was a dinosaur?" JT asked.

"The what?" Micky asked.

"The behemoth." Jonas nodded toward JT. "That's what I was going to mention. Near the end of the Book of Job, God describes two creatures in great detail. The first one is called behemoth and the other is the leviathan. The behemoth is very interesting because the description of it matches only one animal that we know of." He paused and held out a hand to encourage one of the teens to reply.

"I suppose you're going to say a dinosaur," Izzy said.

"That's right. A sauropod or longneck dinosaur, to be exact. God describes the behemoth as having a huge, powerful stomach, bones like bars of iron, and a tail like a cedar tree. Sadly, many study Bibles claim that this creature was probably an elephant or a hippopotamus, but it could not have been either of those."

"Why not?" Izzy asked.

"Well, first of all, neither of those animals has a tail that would remind anyone of a cedar tree. Some people will argue that the word translated as tail could also mean trunk. Although it is never translated that way in the Bible, even if it could be, it still wouldn't make any sense, because the last verse in that chapter says that he has a nose. An elephant doesn't have a nose. Plus, it also says that no one but God can capture it. So it is clearly not referring to an elephant or hippopotamus."

"Okay, so if that's true, then what happened to them?" Izzy asked.

"Well, I would say the Flood wiped out most of them. Then when they got off the Ark, the environment probably made it tougher for them to survive. They wouldn't have had as much food right away, so it's unlikely that they repopulated much."

Jonas took a quick sip. "I think that hunters or knights finished off most of the rest of them. Think about all those stories from long ago about knights slaying dragons. Were those all just made up, or could some of them have been about real people who fought what we would call dinosaurs?"

"And there are stories like that from all over the world, right?" JT asked.

"From every continent except Antarctica.

There's a lot of physical evidence that supports the idea that man has lived with dinosaurs. We have cave drawings of dinosaurs. There's an ancient temple in Southeast Asia that has a carving of what looks like a stegosaurus. In Carlisle Cathedral in England, there's a five-hundred-year-old crypt that has several dinosaurs carved into it. How would the people who drew or carved these things know what dinosaurs looked like? The first dinosaur fossils weren't unearthed until the early 1800s. The best explanation is that they saw living dinosaurs."

"Hold on a sec," Micky said. "You said that dinosaurs got off the Ark. So how did the behemoth that you just told us about fit on the Ark in the first place?"

"You know, Micky, I'm glad you brought that up. That's a great question, too," Jonas said. "Did you know that the average size of an adult dinosaur was only about the size of a bison?"

"Really? You're kidding, right?"

"No, I'm serious." Jonas took a long drink. "Many were actually quite small, and even the largest dinosaurs, like behemoth, started out small. Noah would have probably taken younger animals for many reasons. They would have taken up less space, eaten less food, and would have had more years to reproduce after they got off the Ark.

"Plus, the Ark was enormous. It was longer

than a football field and had the capacity of about four hundred fifty railroad boxcars. It's been estimated that all of the animals could have fit in just over a third of the Ark. That would leave plenty of room for food and living space for the animals and people."

Jax bit into his burger without taking his eyes off of Jonas. He couldn't believe he had never heard of any of these arguments before. *JT is right. The Bible can explain dinosaurs and so much more.* He looked quickly at his friends. Izzy seemed to be hanging on every word. JT was smiling, but Micky sat straight-faced, and Jax couldn't tell what she was thinking.

"Ladies," William said as he and Ted walked toward their table again. "So, Micky, we were just talking about it. Since we totally destroyed your floating bear, we decided that we should buy you and JT some dessert. Sound good?"

"It's about time you did something to make up for that," Micky said.

"Just wait until you hear the best part." William put his hand on Ted's shoulder. "You get the pleasure of our company."

"That's right. We'll do it as long as we get to sit over here and talk with Mr. Ellis." Ted looked at Jonas. "Don't worry, we'll buy yours, too."

Jonas smiled. "With an offer like that, how can I refuse?"

"What about us?" Jax asked as he pointed to himself and Izzy.

"You're on your own, dudes," William said.

Jax pulled the car into the driveway and pushed the button on the garage door opener. He noticed a package lying inside and could make out the name of the company on the package. "Hey, Micky, we got the part for the hoverboard."

"Really? Are you sure?" She leaned over the front seat to get a better look.

"Of course I'm sure." He pulled into the garage and had barely stopped the car when Micky hopped out of the back seat. She ran over to the package and picked it up.

"Yep, it's from Tosche," she said. "Now we can get that thing working."

Jonas pulled into the driveway and parked. He rolled down his window and, in a raised voice, asked, "So do you want to show me that car now or once we get to the observatory?"

"Let's wait 'til we get there," Jax said.

"Hey, guys," Micky said as she held up the hoverboard. "Let's take this, too. We can hook up the new power converter and try it out."

EIGHT

"That's so cool," Micky said as she gazed into the eyepiece of the giant telescope. She was looking directly into the night sky at the Morris-Faulkner Comet.

"C'mon, Micky. Let somebody else take a turn," Jax said.

"Just wait a minute. You'll get a chance. This is just amazing. I can't believe how much detail you can see."

The four teens stood with Jonas beneath one of the largest telescopes in the world at the Foot-hills Observatory.

"So how often does this comet pass by Earth?" Izzy asked.

"Well, its orbital period is 150 years," Jonas said. "So it actually passes by Earth twice every 150 years. It will be a bit closer in October after it goes around the sun and heads back."

"Wait..." Izzy said. "Is it exactly 150 years, or is it like 150 years and 3 months or something like that?"

Jonas closed his eyes and scratched his cheek. "I'm not really sure, but I can check." He walked over to the row of desks and sat down at one of the computers. As he typed, he asked, "Why do you want to know that?"

Before Izzy could answer, Jax asked, "Are you thinking what I'm thinking?"

"It says here that the orbital period is 149 years, 364 ¾ days."

"That's perfect," Izzy said.

"What's perfect? What are you guys talking about?"

"Well, we told you before that we programmed the time machine to go back exactly 4,500 years. If it really went back to that time, then we should be able to see the same comet."

JT, who had been standing at the telescope humming to herself, whipped her head around at Izzy's statement. "That's a great idea. We totally have to go."

Jax grimaced and ground his teeth in frustration. *I wish I could talk her out of it. But if the last trip didn't change her mind, nothing will.*

Micky stepped away from the telescope and clapped excitedly. "Yeah, let's go tonight."

Jonas stood up, his eyes wide and sparkling. "You realize that I'm coming too, right? After all, you're my responsibility tonight."

Jax cleared his throat. "Um…I think you guys are forgetting something."

"What's that?" Micky asked.

"Well, it's not like we've had a good safety record so far. We've been in life-and-death situations both times." He looked right at JT but spoke to the group. "Aren't you at least a little concerned about going back again?"

The girls shook their heads. "Not really," JT said. "We can make it a very quick trip and just hover the whole time." She paused momentarily before continuing. "Well, I guess we'd have to get out for a little bit if we wanted to look at the sky. But we can just go to our previous entry point. We should be safe there."

"Yeah, that would probably work," Izzy said. "Have you charged the battery, Jax?"

"Yeah, we'll have plenty of power. I just think we should be a little more cautious."

"Jax, you're such a baby," Micky said.

Jax crossed his arms. "That's easy for you to say. You haven't been up close and personal with Al yet."

"No, but that huge croc almost got me."

"Hey, Jax," Jonas said. His eyes had returned to normal. "If you think it's too dangerous, let's not do it. Don't feel obligated to do it just because I want to go."

"Yeah, that goes for me, too," JT said. "We did agree that we have to reach a unanimous decision before taking any trips."

Jax could hear the disappointment in her voice and see it on her face. He ran his fingers through his spiked hair and then let out a deep sigh. "No, it's fine. I'm cool with it. I just want to make sure that we're careful. But I think JT's plan sounds good. We'll just go back to the same place we entered last time and stay on that ridge."

"Alright. What are we waiting for?" Micky asked as she jumped up and down.

"Hold on. You're the only one who's seen the comet so far, and I'm taking a look at it before we leave," Jax said as he walked past Micky.

"Yeah, me too," JT said.

"Well, I guess while we're waiting, I might as well teach you something about comets," Jonas said. "Did you know they actually provide some powerful evidence that the universe is not billions of years old?"

"What?" Jax asked as he peered through the telescope. "How?"

"Think about it," Jonas said. "What is the tail of the comet made of?"

"It's bits and pieces of the head breaking off," Izzy said.

"Exactly. Many scientists believe that comets are billions of years old, but every time a comet makes its pass by the sun, it loses a large amount of material. As you know, this can't go on forever. It's been estimated that short-term comets like this one could only last for about ten thousand years. The long-term ones, which have a much longer orbital period, could probably last about ten times that. But either way, they cannot be billions, or even millions, of years old."

"Well, then how come scientists still say that

90

the universe is billions of years old?" Micky asked.

Jax stepped away from the telescope to give Jonas his full attention.

"Good question," Jonas said. "The answer is that they have developed what we call a rescuing device. Whenever there is evidence that seems to go against their theory, they develop a rescuing device to save it. In this case, many scientists believe in something called the Oort Cloud. This is allegedly the birthing place of long-term comets."

"So if the Oort Cloud is where they come from, how does that support the young Earth idea?" Micky asked.

"The problem is that nobody has ever seen the Oort Cloud. As far as we know, it doesn't exist. It might, but other than the fact that comets exist, there is no evidence for it. That's why I called it a rescuing device. Some scientists came up with it to save their theory."

Jonas closed the lid on his laptop and unplugged it. "To be fair, though, everyone comes up with rescuing devices—even creationists. Some rescuing devices are better than others because they are better supported by the evidence. Some are actually proven to be right at some point in the future. But as it stands now, the existence of comets is a strong argument for a young Earth and universe."

"So how in the world did a couple of high school students build this?" Jonas asked as they walked toward the time machine.

"Actually, it was my dad's idea. He drew up most of the plans, but Izzy and I built it."

"Why didn't your dad do it?"

Jax looked down. "He was killed a few years ago in an accident. I found his plans in some old college notebooks, so we decided to go for it."

Jonas put his hand on Jax's shoulder. "I'm sorry, Jax. I didn't know."

Jax unlocked the car doors with his remote control. "That's alright. I think I'm finally coming to grips with it since getting right with God."

"I'm glad to hear that."

"I have to hook that cable back up, or we're not going anywhere. Um…are there any security cameras around here?" Jax asked.

"Yeah, there's one pointed straight at this parking lot. You could pull around to the side of the building, though. There aren't any cameras over there."

"Sounds good to me. Everyone hop in."

Jonas and the girls climbed into the back. Jax noticed that Jonas was staring at the electronic equipment covering the dash. "So what do you think?"

"It looks pretty cool," Jonas said. "But how do you operate it?"

"Well, I actually control most of it from here," Izzy said as he booted up the computer. "I'll select the date, time, and coordinates of our destination. Then it's just a click of the button, and we're outta here."

Jax put the key in the ignition, fired up the car, then drove out of the security camera's view. "How are we doing, Iz?"

"Almost there. Do we just want to go back to the same day that we left before, but just later at night?"

"I think so, but make sure you put us in at the previous entry point rather than at the top of the waterfall."

"How about if you give us an hour or two of daylight so that we can hover around and show Jonas what it looks like there?" Micky asked. "Maybe he'll even get to see a dinosaur."

"No problem. That's a good idea." Izzy clicked the laptop's touchpad a few more times. "The coordinates are all set."

Jax stopped the car and hopped out. "Izzy, can you give me a hand with the cable?"

"Sure."

Jax opened the trunk and pushed the large cable through the hole in the top. Izzy pulled it forward to the front of the roof and attached it. The boys got back into the car and fastened their seat belts.

"Alright," Izzy said. "Is everyone ready?"

"I'm not sure," Jonas said as he clenched the seat belt. "Should I be nervous?"

"Don't worry," JT said. "It doesn't hurt at all. You'll just see a quick flash of light, and that's it."

"Thanks. That's good to know."

"Alright. Here we go," Izzy said.

The time machine's countdown began. After the computer said "one," light filled the car's interior. When Jax opened his eyes again, the observatory was gone.

NINE

"This looks like the right spot," Jax said. He looked into the rear-view mirror. "Is everybody okay?"

Pale-faced and staring at the scene in front of him, Jonas said, "This is unreal. I can't believe it. You actually did it."

"Yeah, time travel is awesome, but there's more," Micky said. "We told you this thing hovers, too."

Izzy reached for the sliding levels on the dash. "Hang on." He slowly slid the levels up a touch, and the car rose about a foot off the ground. He stopped and looked at Jonas.

"You guys, this is incredible! I'm back in time, and I'm hovering in a car. How high can it go?"

"Let me show you," Izzy said as he slid the levels up a little farther. As he did, the car rose awkwardly. The back right lifted up, but the front left stayed closer to the ground. Izzy looked puzzled. "What's going on?"

Just then Jax heard a loud snap, and the car jerked violently.

JT screamed.

"Put it down!" Jax yelled.

Izzy slid the levels all the way down. The car wobbled as it descended and soon came to rest with a thud.

"What happened?" Micky asked.

Jax was already opening his door. "I don't know, but I'm going to find out." He stood up and surveyed the ground beneath him. The other car doors opened as his friends exited the vehicle too. Then Jax saw it. "Oh no. Not good."

"What is it?" JT asked.

He pointed down to the area just behind the front left tire. "The repulsor—"

"You broke it," Micky said.

One of her hovering devices lay on the ground, wedged underneath a tree root. Jax bent down and grabbed it.

"What happened?" Izzy asked.

"It looks like this tree root must have been wrapped around it." Jax kicked at the root. "Of all the places to enter, we had to come in right in this exact spot."

"But why didn't we notice it right away when you started making us hover?" Micky asked as she looked at Izzy.

He bent down and took hold of the root. As he pulled up, it rose about two feet before it stopped. "I guess it was just loose enough to let us go up that high, but as soon as we tried going higher, it tightened."

JT picked up the device and cradled it as she sat on the ground. "So how come it didn't do that last time?"

"I don't know," Izzy said. "Maybe we didn't appear in the exact same spot. Or maybe it was on there and just slipped off."

"Or maybe we uprooted it when we hovered last time," Jax said.

Micky put her hands on her hips. "It doesn't really matter why it didn't happen last time. What do we do now?"

Jax got on his back and scooted under the car. "Wait, it looks like it just popped out of its housing." He scrambled to his feet, went to the back of the car, and popped the trunk. "Izzy and I can fix this in no time."

"You want to fix it here?" JT asked.

"Sure, why not? I've got my tools." He grunted as he pulled them out of the trunk. "Besides, it will give you guys a chance to point out where we've been."

"That sounds good," Jonas said.

"Oh, I almost forgot," Jax said. "Micky, you could get going on this." He grinned as he handed her the box that held the new power converter.

Micky's face lit up. "Oh yeah, this is gonna be awesome." Reaching into the trunk, she pulled out the snowboard that already had both repulsors installed and grabbed a few tools to finish the job.

"Can you work on that over here?" JT asked as she walked toward the edge of the ridge.

"Sure thing. C'mon Jonas. We'll tell you more

about this place as we work."

He walked toward the girls and then stopped and looked back at Jax and Izzy. "Are you sure you guys don't need any help?"

"Nah, go ahead," Izzy said. "We got this."

"And way downstream was the waterfall," JT said while pointing to her left while Jonas looked on.

"Finished," Micky said.

"What? Done already?" JT jumped up. "Guess it's time for a test run."

"Yep." Micky set the board on the ground. "Hand me the remote. I'm first."

"I thought we could both try it at the same time," JT said as she stepped on the board near the front.

"Okay." Micky stepped onto the back of the board. "Let's do it."

JT flipped the power switch on the remote. A small red light shone from the front of the board. "Here we go." She slowly turned one dial, and the board shimmied for a couple of seconds. As she turned the dial further, the board slowly lifted off the ground. "It's working."

"Yeah, we did it," Micky said and then reached forward and hugged JT. As she shifted her weight, the board teetered slightly. She looked at Jonas. "What do you think?"

He stared at the board, which was nearly a

foot above the ground. "That's incredible. How do you get it to move?"

JT looked over her shoulder at him. "It's pretty much the same principle as the repulsors under the car. If we want to go forward, the back one will tilt to propel us. Watch."

Suddenly, the board shot forward, throwing Micky off balance. Too late, she tried to grab JT to steady herself. JT reached back, but their hands met only momentarily before Micky lost her grip, slipped off the board, and fell awkwardly to the ground.

JT maintained her balance. Within a few seconds, she managed to complete a U-turn and headed back. Slowly powering down the device, she stopped just a few feet from where Jonas was helping Micky to her feet. With a huge smile on her face, she said, "I guess that was a successful test run."

Micky dusted some dirt from her elbow and smiled. "You little brat. You did that on purpose."

JT was still beaming. "Of course I did. It's not my fault you couldn't stay on." She stepped off the board and handed the remote to Micky. "Your turn."

"That should do it," Jax said as he stood and brushed his hands off.

Izzy also got up, and they started walking toward the others. Izzy looked up at the sky and sighed, "It doesn't look like we'll get to see that comet tonight."

Jax had been so busy with repairing the repulsor that he hadn't noticed the ominous storm clouds that had rolled in. "Ah man, that stinks. We could just jump ahead another day if we wanted."

"That's true, but first I gotta wash all this gunk off my hands," Izzy said while lifting his greasy left hand up in front of Jax's face.

"Yeah, me too."

"Watch out," Micky said.

Jax jumped to the side as she zipped past him on the hoverboard. "Hey, it's working."

Micky slowed the board and stepped off. "Of course it's working."

"That's sweet," Izzy said. "We'll have to try it out after we get cleaned up."

"Hey Jax," Jonas called. Grinning, he pointed to where the teens had first encountered the allosaurus. "Micky told me that you and Izzy wanted to go explore that ridge over there."

"Yeah, right. Maybe she can be your tour guide. There's no way I'm going over there again."

"That's for sure," Izzy said. "But we do need to head down to the river."

"What, right now?" JT asked. "It's getting dark, and it feels like a storm is rolling in."

"It's only going to take a few minutes," Jax said. "We'll be right back."

Jax and Izzy ambled down the steep ridge and then across the small field to the river's edge. A steady rain began falling just before they reached the river. As Jax knelt down and plunged his hands into the water, a stiff breeze kicked up from the north and the rain started flying sideways, pelting the boys in the face.

"Man, it sure got dark fast," Jax yelled over the howling wind. "We'd better hurry."

Izzy knelt down and feverishly rubbed his hands together in the water. "Yeah, it's getting nasty out here."

Jax turned to look back at the rest of their group and noticed they were no longer visible.

Izzy jumped up and shouted, "Let's get out of here." Jax continued scrubbing his hands for a few more seconds. "Come on, Jax!"

He sprang to his feet. "Alright, I'm coming."

"Whew," Micky said as she shut her door. "That came on quick. The boys are gonna be soaked."

"They'd better hurry up," JT said. "It looks pretty bad out there already."

"Where are they?" Micky asked. "I can't even see them anymore. It's too dark."

"Why don't we drive over to the edge and turn on the lights? Then they could at least see us," Jonas said.

"Good idea," Micky said as she climbed into the driver's seat. She started the car, turned on the headlights, and drove close the ledge.

"Where are they?" JT asked.

TEN

The boys ran back across the small field and arrived at the base of the ridge. The landing spot was only about twenty feet above them. Izzy climbed about five feet before he lost his footing and slid back down, almost wiping Jax out in the process.

"Sorry, it's already really slick." He started to climb again, but stopped and pointed. "Look."

Jax looked in the direction Izzy was pointing. "They must have driven to the edge to give us some light. Here, let me try."

Jax carefully started to make his way up the slope. To help balance himself, he grabbed some of the long grass as he tried to negotiate the hillside. He made it to about the same spot as Izzy had moments earlier when he lost his footing and slid down the hill. "We have to get up there before it gets any worse."

Izzy took a couple of steps back and then tried running up the incline. He had only made it a few feet up when his foot failed to gain any traction. He slipped and fell forward, but he managed to catch himself before burying his face in the mud. He climbed to his feet and looked at Jax. "There's no way we can make it up in this weather."

"Hey, we're down here!" Jax yelled at the top of his lungs, hoping someone in the car would hear him.

"I'm going out to look for them," JT said.

Micky looked back. "Girl, you can't go out in this weather. They'll be here soon enough. Just wait a little longer."

"Micky's right," Jonas said. They can't be too far away. We just saw them at the river's edge."

JT climbed forward into the passenger seat. "Maybe we can go look for them." She reached for the levels to control the hover devices.

"JT, I don't think that's such a—" Jonas' comment came a second too late. She had already slid the levels up, raising the car several feet. A strong gust of wind caught the underbelly of the car.

The girls screamed as the time machine was thrown back away from the edge of the ridge. JT reached for the dashboard to steady herself, but accidentally bumped one of the levels. The right side of the car lurched upward, and the wind sent them spinning out of control.

Micky clutched the steering wheel. "Bring us down!"

"I'm trying." JT was thrown back and forth a few times before managing to grab her seat belt and strap in. She reached for the joystick and the levels.

Just as she grabbed the controls, the car suddenly shot higher in the air. JT's stomach plummeted.

Jonas gripped the seat behind her. "What's going on?"

The sudden jolt caused JT to lose her grip on

the levels again. She was still clinging to the joystick, and she fought to steady the car, but it was no use as long as the wind was buffeting it. "I think we just flew over the top of the ridge that was behind us."

With great effort, she reached forward. *Got it. Better not slide them down too quickly or we'll crash.* The car plunged until it was hovering just a few feet above the ground. The wind was still blowing hard, but it didn't have the same effect now that the car was so low. She slowly slid the levels down the rest of the way, and the car finally came to rest.

Micky took a deep breath. "That was too close."

"Are you girls okay?" Jonas asked.

"I'm alright," Micky said. "JT?"

JT shook uncontrollably. *This is all my fault. I should have known it was too windy to hover. Oh no. The guys are still out there.* She buried her face in her hands and sobbed. "They'll never find us up here."

"The cave," Jax said.

"What are you talking about?" Izzy asked.

"That cave that Micky found when we were exploring. We can stay in there."

"Oh yeah. Where is it?"

"This way." Jax ran around the front of the ridge and then west in the direction of the waterfall. "It wasn't too far away from here. Just keep your eyes peeled."

They moved along, looking for the cave that they hoped would provide shelter to ride out the storm. Fierce gusts of wind prevented them from running quickly. The raindrops hit so hard that Jax felt like he was being pelted with paintballs.

"Is that it?" Izzy asked, pointing.

"I think so. Let's go."

They soon came to the mouth of the cave. Stooping down, they entered the blackness before them.

"Do you have a flashlight?" Izzy asked.

Jax pulled out his new cell phone and pushed a button that sent a faint blue glow into the darkness before them. He held it out in front of him and gradually moved deeper into the cave. "I sure hope we're alone in here."

"Yeah," Izzy said as he shivered. "Me too."

The rain was blowing into the cave, but the boys had moved far enough back that they were no longer in it. Izzy dug into his pocket and pulled out his phone. He flipped it open and said, "Let's go a little farther and find some dry ground."

They continued moving slowly through the cave, which soon widened to about three paces across. "This looks good," Jax said. "Let's rest here for a while and see if that storm calms down at all."

"Sounds good to me."

They sat down and Jax scooted back against one wall. Izzy slid back to lean against the opposite wall and said, "We have to let them know that we're okay."

"I'll try paging them." Jax punched a few buttons on his phone. As he pressed the appropriate button, his phone bleeped. They waited for several seconds, but there was no response. He tried again, but there was still no response.

"Maybe the roof of this cave is too thick for the signal to get through. We'll have to try outside," Izzy said.

"I'm not going back out there yet. Let's give it a few minutes. I'm just gonna close my eyes and rest for a bit. When it dies down, I'll try calling again."

He squirmed against the wall to get comfortable. "You know, I'm sick of all the mishaps every time we're here. Still…did you see the look on Jonas' face when we appeared on that ridge?"

"Yeah, it's pretty cool that someone like him would be amazed at something we did." Izzy yawned. "I never pictured one of the top scientists being a Christian."

Jax pondered that as the adrenaline rush of getting through the storm wore off. *Yeah, he really seems to have answers. It looks like JT has been right all along.* Within a few minutes, he drifted off to sleep.

"I'm just gonna leave the lights on so they can find us," Micky said.

"I don't know if it will do any good. We're all the way on top of the ridge now, and they'll never look here," JT said.

Micky placed her hand on JT's shoulder. "It's all we can do. If the battery dies, we can charge it in the morning."

"It's not the only thing we can do," Jonas said. "We can pray for their safety."

JT closed her eyes. "Would you please?"

"Absolutely."

After the prayer they talked about other issues to pass the time. The rain pounded steadily on the car for another half hour before slowing to a soothing rhythm, and eventually Micky and Jonas fell asleep.

JT wished she could sleep, but her mind was filled with worry. *God, please keep Jax and Izzy safe tonight, wherever they are. Thank You so much for Jax coming to faith and for letting me answer some of his questions.* The image of Jax's smiling face filled her thoughts for a moment. She made a conscious effort to keep praying. *Please use him to make a difference in Izzy's and Micky's life, too. They both need You so desperately.*

Her mind drifted to Jax again, and this time she didn't force the image away. *If this is just a ruse to get me to like him, he sure is doing a good*

job of acting. No, there is no doubt, he's a true be-
liever. That final thought brought a smile to her
face for the first time since the storm started, and
she eventually succumbed to sleep.

"Hey, wake up."

Jax jerked, and his elbow hit something hard.
He moaned and tried to force his eyes open as
Izzy shook him. He had fallen asleep while sitting
down, his back against the cave wall, his knees
pulled up close to his chest, his arms folded and
resting on his knees, and his head on his arms.

"C'mon, the sun's up. We slept all night. Jonas
and the girls are probably freaking out. We have
to get back to the car."

Jax sat up abruptly, and his head banged into
the wall. "Ouch!" Unfolding himself, he tried to
stretch out because his body ached from sleeping
in such an awkward position. "Okay, I'm up."

They climbed to their feet and crept toward
the light at the mouth of the cave. As he emerged,
Jax jumped over a large puddle. When he landed
on the soggy ground, muddy water splashed onto
his pant legs. The sun had just cleared the horizon, and no cloud was in the sky. A cool, gentle
breeze rifled through his hair.

They were soon at the base of the steep hill
again. "I hope it's dry enough to get up," Jax said.

"It still looks really slick."

"Yeah, but at least we can see where we're stepping now."

The boys carefully made their way up the steep incline. They slipped a couple of times but were able to make it up. Covered with mud, Jax reached the ledge first and looked around. "Where's the car?"

Izzy had just reached the top, and disappointment came over his face. "They must have gone to look for us. Hey, try your phone again."

Jax pulled out his phone. It was dead. "Stink. I left it on last night, and the battery ran down."

Izzy checked his phone. "Mine too. That figures."

"Do you want to wait here or should we try to find them?"

"I'm not even sure where I would start to look."

Jax turned a full circle and considered the landmarks around them. "How 'bout downstream, toward the waterfall? Since we were by the river when all the rain started, they might be concerned that we got carried downstream."

Izzy shrugged. "Okay, I don't have any better ideas. Let's go."

"Hold on," JT said. "This might get pretty bumpy." The time machine lurched as it coasted over the ridge. She nudged the levels back and forth to ease their descent as she successfully navigated to the bottom of the ridge.

Micky had made it down first and was zipping around on the hoverboard.

"You've really gotten the hang of that," Jonas shouted through the open driver's side window.

Micky laughed and started showing off. She leaned to her left and spun one of the remote's wheels. The board shot out from underneath her as she tumbled to the ground. The board soon came to a stop a few feet away.

JT shook her head and smiled. She never learns.

"Are you okay?" Jonas asked.

She pushed herself off the ground and walked over to the hoverboard. "Yep, gotta get back on that horse."

"It's a good thing you installed a cutoff switch," JT said. "Otherwise, we'd be chasing that board all over the place."

Micky hovered over to the passenger side of the car and leaned over to talk to JT. She grabbed the door to keep her balance. "So we follow the river downstream to the waterfall, and if we don't see any sign of them we split up?"

"I think that's as good a plan as—" JT stopped as she brightened with hope. "Wait. Remember that cave? Maybe they stayed in there."

Micky looked puzzled for a second, then stood up straight. "Great idea."

Micky took off on the hoverboard, and JT soon had the time machine following her.

"There it is!" Micky shouted and pointed to the opening of the cave. She slowed down, and JT guided the time machine alongside of her.

Jonas pointed down to the ground next to the cave's entrance. "Look, there are footprints in the mud here."

They jumped out of the car and ran to the tracks. Micky stepped off the hoverboard, and soon all three bent down to examine the footprints.

"Notice the tracks going in are nearly washed away, but the ones leading out are clearly marked," JT said.

"That would mean that they made it here last night and left after the rain stopped," Micky said.

The guys made it through the storm, but where are they? She reached over and hugged Micky. "They're alive." She let go of her friend, cupped her hands to her mouth, and yelled. "Jax! Izzy!"

Micky grabbed her arm. "Girl, remember there are dinosaurs out here."

"Check this out," Jonas said. "The tracks lead back the way we came." He followed the tracks for several yards, stooped low to the ground for a few seconds, and then walked back toward the time machine. "There's another set of tracks leading downstream."

JT pursed her lips. "What does that mean?

Which way did they go?"

"Look," he said as he pointed toward the tracks near the cave. "Like Micky said, the tracks that are nearly washed away indicate the guys made it here last night. But the tracks heading back to our entry point seem to indicate they got up this morning and went back there. Of course, when they arrived, we weren't there. They probably assumed we were already out looking for them. So it looks like they came back this way and kept walking downstream."

"What are we waiting for?" JT asked as she ran toward the car.

"Did you ever imagine it would be like this?" Izzy asked.

Jax turned his gaze from the woods to look at him. "What do you mean?"

"You know, time travel." Izzy swept his arm in a large arc. "I mean, look at this place, it's so full of vegetation. Based on everything we were taught, I thought we'd only see ferns and evergreens."

Jax saw a bird nesting in what looked like an oak tree. A large patch of wildflowers showed off their bright colors in a sunny spot to their left. "No, I gotta admit, almost everything about these trips has been very different than I expected. And I definitely didn't think we would find out that the Bible is right about our past."

"Yeah, about that. How—" A rustling in the forest on the other side of the river grabbed his attention. "What was that?"

"I don't know. Come on."

They ran toward the edge of the forest and ducked in behind a couple of trees. The rustling grew louder. Jax looked across the water and saw several high branches shaking.

"Do you think it's that allosaurus again?" Izzy asked.

Jax shrugged. "If it is, I sure hope he can't swim."

Seconds later, a large dinosaur emerged from the forest. Jax let out a sigh of relief as he realized it wasn't Al. It was a parasauralophus. "Hey, that's probably the same one that JT and I saw last month. Let's check it out."

"Hold on. Don't scare it away. Let's just watch it."

The dinosaur walked to the edge of the river, looked both ways, and sniffed the air. After a few seconds, it looked back toward the forest and honked. Immediately, two smaller dinosaurs appeared from the woods and walked toward their mother. They reached the river and bent down to drink.

"That's what we saw before," Jax said. "The mom and two little ones. Cool, huh?"

Izzy stared wide-eyed. "It's awesome."

The dinosaurs continued to drink for several

moments until the adult stood up tall and stared upstream. The youngsters soon followed their mother's example.

"What are they looking at?" Jax asked.

"I don't know, and I'm not sure if I want to find out."

ELEVEN

"Wow, look at that." Micky slowed the hoverboard to a halt and motioned for JT to do the same with the car.

A large crested dinosaur and two smaller ones drank from the river. "Micky, those are the para… para…aghhh, I can never remember their names," JT said. "Aren't they incredible?"

Micky hopped off the board and walked backward to the car, never taking her eyes off the creatures by the river. "Is it safe to be out here?"

"It should be," JT said. "They're plant-eaters. C'mon, let's get a better look."

Jonas sat staring ahead when JT got out. She shut her door quietly and poked her head in the open window. "What's the matter, Mr. Ellis, haven't you ever seen a dinosaur before?"

Without taking his eyes off the dinosaurs, he said, "Not one with skin on it."

JT grinned. "Come on. Let's go get a better look."

As the girls and Jonas came closer, the adult parasauralophus stood upright and looked directly at them.

JT took a few deliberate steps while all three dinosaurs watched. After a few seconds, the mother bent down and took another drink.

"They aren't running away," Micky whispered.

"No, I don't even think they're afraid of us," Jonas said.

"So how big do you think the adult is?" Micky asked.

JT tried to compare the dinosaurs to the nearby trees when some movement to her left caught her attention. She spun and rubbed her eyes.

"I'm not sure," Jonas said. I would guess—"

"Jax!" JT yelled. She sprinted toward him and Izzy, who was following close behind.

The dinosaurs bounded back into the woods on all fours.

Jax slowed to a walk, but JT threw her arms out and slammed into him. She hugged him as tightly as she could. "I was so worried about you guys," she said as her eyes filled with tears of joy.

He returned the embrace. "I was worried too."

She gave him another tight squeeze, then hugged Izzy, who had just joined them. Jonas and Micky arrived just after Izzy.

When the hugs and handshakes were finished, Jonas asked, "So did you guys stay in that cave?"

"Yep," Izzy said. "It wasn't too bad. We went looking for you this morning, but you weren't there. Where did you go?"

"That's a long story," Micky said. "Let's get back to the car first."

They walked toward the time machine. Still fighting back tears of relief and joy, JT looked at

Jax. "You know, last night, during that storm, I couldn't help but think that maybe we were witnessing the beginning of the Genesis flood and that…" She paused to wipe tears from her eyes. "And that you guys were…"

Jax put one arm around her and gave her a quick hug. "It's okay. We're fine, and pretty soon we'll be safe at home again."

Jonas turned and looked at JT. "I wasn't trying to eavesdrop, but I heard you mention the Flood."

"Yeah, I guess I was so afraid that the guys weren't going to make it that I let my imagination go crazy."

"Well, I can understand your concern," Jonas said. "That was a pretty wicked storm, but it was nothing compared to what the start of the Flood would have been."

"What do you mean?" JT asked.

"The Bible says that the fountains of the great deep broke open at the start of the Flood. I think that means there was all kinds of volcanic and geyser activity in addition to all the rain. If it was the Flood, it would have been far beyond anything we've ever experienced."

Izzy cleared his throat. "You really believe that stuff about the Flood and Noah's Ark, don't you?"

"I do," Jonas said. "The Bible says it, so that settles it. But we also have abundant evidence to show there was a worldwide flood." He bit his bottom lip for a moment. "You know, we could prove it if you guys wanted to."

"Really? How?" Micky asked as the group reached the time machine.

"Well, you guys built a time machine, right?" He said as he slapped the hood of the car. "If your calculations are right, we're some one hundred to one hundred and fifty years before the Flood."

"So we could just travel about two hundred years from now and check it out," Jax said.

"That's right," Jonas said. "If the Bible's accurate, and there was a worldwide flood, it would have completely changed the landscape of the entire world. That means this area will look drastically different than it does now. But, if the Flood and Ark are just fairy tales, like so many think, then we should expect this place to look pretty much the same."

"That's a great idea," Jax said. "What do you think guys? Should we do it?"

JT and Izzy were quick to agree with him. Micky looked down and hesitated, then said, "Yeah, that sounds okay."

"Great, let's go," Jax said.

As they piled in, Jonas asked, "So this thing can hover over water, right?"

"Whoa," Jax said.

Micky stared out her window. *I can't believe*

this. It can't be the same place. The landscape was vastly different than before. *Where are all the trees?* A few small trees and some scattered grasses and shrubs dotted the terrain. There was no sign of any people or animals in the bleak countryside.

Izzy punched a few keys on the computer. "I'm double-checking the coordinates to make sure this is the same spot." He stared at the screen in disbelief.

"So is it?" JT asked.

"Yes. At least, that's what the computer says," Izzy said as he turned to look out his window.

As the others talked about how this latest development supported the Bible, Micky tried to make sense of the scene before her. *I only agreed to this because I thought it would prove the Bible wrong once and for all. But this...* As she gazed out at the desolate landscape, something deep within her revolted. *No. The computer's wrong. They're all wrong.*

"Micky, did you hear me?" Jax said.

Micky jumped. "What?"

"I asked what you thought of all this."

Micky tried her best not to show her frustration. *I just want to go home, but I need to keep them off my back.* "You know, if we are in the post-Flood world right now, there's a danger that someone might see us and we'll end up impacting the future in some way. We should probably get going right away."

"But we just got here," Jax said.

"Jax," Jonas said. "I think Micky's right. We should probably go. We already saw what we needed to see."

Jax nodded. "I understand. Izzy, take us home."

TWELVE

"See you guys on Monday," Micky said as she got out of the car, following the near-silent drive from the observatory.

"Later," Jax said while Izzy and JT also said their good-byes to her.

Jax put the car in reverse and backed out of her driveway. As they pulled away, he looked at Izzy and then at JT in the rearview mirror. "That was quite a trip."

"Yeah, it's hard to believe everything we've been through," JT said.

"So what was your favorite thing that we've seen?" Jax asked.

"I don't know. There's so much to choose from." She sat up straight. "It's pretty cool that we saw real dinosaurs, but I especially loved how everything was perfectly consistent with the Bible. What about you, Izzy? What was your favorite part?"

Izzy was quiet for a moment and then asked, "It's all true, isn't it?"

"What are you talking about, Iz?" Jax asked.

"The Bible. It's all true, isn't it?"

Jax could not believe his ears. Was this an answer to prayer? He glanced in the mirror and met JT's wide-eyed gaze. "I believe it is," he said.

Izzy looked at him. "So that means that all the stuff in Genesis is true. And all the things that

Jesus taught are true, right?"

Jax nodded.

"So...what now?" Izzy asked.

Jax remembered being on the other end of a similar discussion just a few weeks earlier. *I'm not an expert and I'm not sure what to say. God, please give me the right words.*

He pulled the car to the curb and parked while JT scooted forward and leaned between the seats. "Izzy, the things that Jesus taught are true." As soon as he finished the first sentence, he knew exactly what to say. "That means that He came to take your place on the cross. He came to die for your sins, Iz—and mine, too. We all deserve to be separated from God forever, but Jesus came to take our punishment. He wants you to trust in Him, to know Him in a personal way."

Jax paused to give Izzy a chance to reply, but he just sat quietly, paying close attention. His eyes welled up as if he were going to start crying, but no tears flowed.

"Iz, you gotta get right with God," Jax said. "As it stands now, you face His judgment. But if you turn to Him and give Him your life, He'll give you everlasting life."

Izzy looked at JT and then back at Jax. "You're right. What do I need to do?"

Jax's eyes lit up, and he turned in his seat to face his friend. "I'll tell you what Pastor Rich told me when I asked the same question. He said that I needed to put my faith in Jesus Christ alone to save me from my sins. There isn't some magical formula, but just pray to God and tell Him that you believe that Jesus came and died in your place and rose from the dead. Tell Him that you want to live for Him, and ask Him to save you from your sins."

JT placed a hand on Izzy's shoulder. "Would you like us to pray with you?"

He nodded. "Thanks."

Jax reached out to ring the doorbell, then nervously combed his fingers through his spiked hair as he waited.

Seconds later JT opened the door and smiled. "Hey, Jax, this is a nice surprise. What are you doing here?"

He fumbled for the right words. "Well, after everything that's happened, I just wanted to see you."

She blushed and looked down. "Yeah, it has been an amazing weekend."

He sat on the top step of the porch. "I talked to Izzy on the way over. That was awesome earlier today."

"It sure was." She sat beside him. "How is he doing?"

"He wants me to pick him up for church tomorrow."

"That's great," she said as she stared out across the front yard. "It's hard to believe how much things have changed in the last month."

His mind immediately flashed back to the previous month, when they had been sitting in the same spots and she had broken his heart. *She's right. So much has changed. Before, all I cared about was myself and blamed God for everything wrong in my life. Now, I just want to live for Him.* "It sure is. I feel like a different person. You know, I can't thank you enough for all your prayers and for not giving up on me."

She blushed and scooted up against him. "Well, I'm glad Jesus didn't give up on either of us." She rested her head on his shoulder.

Jax smiled broadly and nervously leaned his head on top of hers. As they sat silently, he prayed. *Lord, thank You for Your goodness and for taking away my bitterness. I never understood what true joy was until I gave my life to You. Thank You.*

Time seemed to fly by as they sat there talking and laughing. Jax looked off in the distance and noticed the sun had nearly set. "I can't believe how late it is already."

"Yeah, I should probably go in. We do have church in the morning."

They sat for a few moments in silence before she fidgeted and sat up straight. Then she leaned over and gave him a quick kiss on the cheek.

Jax's jaw dropped, and he looked at her with widened eyes. "What?"

The color in her face deepened as she stood up abruptly. She gave his hair a brief tousle, then turned toward the door. "I... I... I need to go. Um...my dad is speaking at my grandparents' church, so we have to leave early in the morning. I'll see you later?"

"Absolutely," he said. Confusion and elation battled within him. "G'night, JT."

"Good night...Jaxon," A huge smile crossed her face. She turned, entered her house, and closed the door quietly behind her.

Jax stared after her for a moment as a big smile spread across his face. She hadn't said anything was for certain between them, but if this day was any indication of their future, he could hardly wait to see what was in store. He stood up to leave. *This is the best day of my life.*

JT backed up against the door and giggled. *What an awesome day. The hoverboard. Izzy. Jax.* She started humming her favorite song.

"Everything okay, sweetheart?" her father asked as he approached her.

She danced over and wrapped her arms tightly around him. "Everything's perfect."

Jax pulled into his driveway and saw a familiar-looking black sedan. *Not again.* His heart raced, and the peace he had just experienced evaporated. *Why do they have to be here tonight?* He parked, shut off the engine, and hurried to the front door.

He paused when he heard voices from inside. *That's weird. Why are they laughing?* Confused and scared, he took a deep breath, then opened the door and walked in.

As expected, Agents Kimball and Johnson were on the sofa. Jax did a double take at his mom, who sat on the loveseat. She was smiling, and her eyes were wet. They stopped talking when he entered the room.

Before he could ask what was going on, Agent Kimball stood. "I'm sure you're wondering what brings us here tonight. Jax, we have some excellent news for you. We—"

The agent stopped and smiled after someone in the next room cleared his throat.

Jax looked toward the bathroom. *Who else is here?* "Mom, who—"

Just then a man came around the corner. It was his father.

Older, thinner, with more lines around his eyes, but Jax knew those blue eyes as well as his own. He swallowed hard. "Dad?" Jax asked when he found his voice, not willing to trust his eyes, which were rapidly filling with tears. "Is it...is it really you?"

"Jax," his dad said. "I can't tell you how good it is to see you."

With tears now streaming down his cheeks, Jax sprinted to his dad and nearly knocked him to the ground. He hugged him tightly and held on with every ounce of strength he possessed, fearing that his dad would disappear if he let go. "I thought you were dead."

His dad, crying just as hard, hugged him back. "It's okay, son. Everything's going to be alright now."

Soon his mom stood and joined them.

Jax put one arm around her and pulled her close. *This really is the best day of my life.*

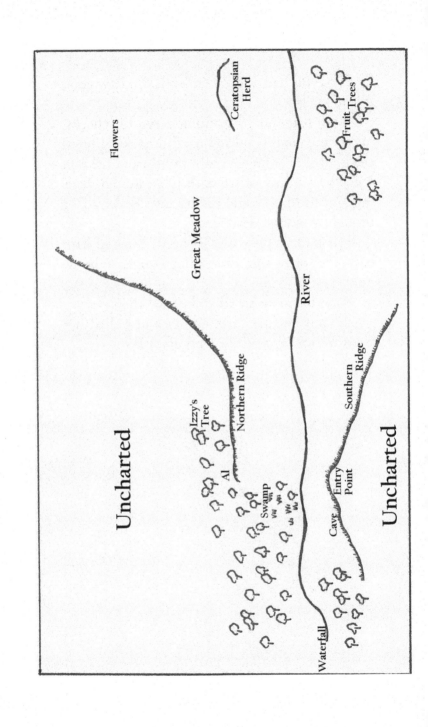

EPILOGUE

Jax yawned. *That was the best I've slept in years. What's that noise? Oh, my phone.* He rolled over and picked it up off the nightstand. It was a text from Izzy: **What time r u picking me up?**

Oh yeah, church. He quickly typed a response: **9:15 and I've got a big surprise.**

He jumped out of bed and hurried out of his room, hoping his dad would be awake. He found his mom and dad sitting at the dining room table, drinking coffee.

"Good morning," Dr. Thompson said.

Jax smiled at the sheer ordinariness of the moment. "I'm so glad it wasn't a dream."

His dad met him with a tight hug. "No, it's all real. I'm home."

Jax looked at his mom, who was smiling wider and looking younger than she had in years. After their embrace, he sat down at the table. "So Dad, you said you were going to tell me all about the escape."

"Oh, Jax, not right now," his mom said. "I'd rather talk about other things."

Jax was anxious to find out what had happened. *I have to know if our video helped at all.*

The disappointment on his face must have been evident, because his dad spoke up. "It's alright, dear. I'd be happy to tell him all about it."

"Sweet," Jax said as he grabbed a plate and dished up some scrambled eggs. "Go ahead."

Dr. Thompson sat up straight and took a sip of his coffee. "Okay. My captors really just wanted the solar cell at the Bureau. But they messed up and caused it to explode, so they kidnapped me to force me to build another one."

Jax's mom grabbed a tissue and wiped her eyes.

"I stalled as long as I could. But when they threatened to harm you guys, I started working on it, but also built a small radio transmitter that could broadcast my old security access code. I didn't expect that anyone would detect it, but it was worth a shot."

Jax reached over and held his mom's hand.

"A couple of weeks later, I was asleep in my room when I was awakened by shouting and gunfire. Several armed men broke into my room and whisked me away. I wasn't sure what was going on. When I was safe aboard a helicopter, one of the men introduced himself as a CIA operative."

"So what happened next?" Jax asked.

"Well, I asked him how they found me, and he said they had received my broadcast. They spent the next two weeks planning the rescue, which obviously went off without a hitch."

Jax finished his bite. "But how did they know to keep looking? Everyone thought you were dead."

"Well, the agent told me that I was very fortunate. They had received an anonymous tip right before my broadcast that led them to the right South American country. If they hadn't directed a bunch of their resources to that area, they never would have been listening when I sent my message."

"Wow, that's amazing," Jax said with a sly grin. He stood and motioned for his dad to follow. "There's something you have to see."

"What is it?" he asked.

"I wanna show you my science fair project."

Jax's father looked at his wife, who was still smiling and wiping a few tears. She nodded and said, "Don't take too long. We still need to get ready for church."

They walked out into the lab. Jax flipped on the lights and walked toward the driver's side door, spreading his arms wide to showcase the beat-up car.

His father looked curiously at the vehicle in front of him and then at Jax. "It can't be."

Jax popped the trunk and reattached the main power cable. "Get in," he said as he climbed into the driver's seat.

Dr. Thompson walked slowly toward the passenger door and sat down. He gazed at the vast array of lights, switches, and other gadgets on the dashboard.

"Jax, did you…did you find my notebooks and solar cell prototypes?" he asked with a knowing smile.

Jax smiled and grabbed the laptop from in front of his dad.

His father stared at him. "It actually works? I mean, I know in theory... but..."

Without saying a word, Jax started the car.

"Where are we going?" He looked at the dashboard and then at the computer on his son's lap. "Or would it be better to ask, when are we going?"

Jax smiled and clicked a few keys to select one of the previous entries. *Let's go back to ten minutes before Izzy and I did so we don't run into ourselves.* He quickly made the change on the computer. "Hold on a minute."

The lights blinked while the Space-Time Generator whirred to life and the countdown began. Jax met his father's gaze just before the countdown finished. "About that anonymous tip..."

THANKS

The authors would like to thank all the people who helped make this series a reality. For their creative input and support, we thank Casey, Abigail, Kayla, Nick, Keith, John, Jevon, Kian, Roger, and Gary.

We want to say a very special thank you to Reagen Reed for her invaluable assistance in editing the series and forcing us to be better writers.

We extend an extra special thank you to Melissa Mathis (a.k.a. Inkhana) for her incredible artwork. Thank you for using your talents for our Lord and Savior Jesus Christ and for your efforts to glorify Him through the use of Manga. If you like the illustrations in this series please visit Melissa's website at www.christianmanga.com and be sure to check out her books.

Finally, we thank Jesus Christ for loving us so much that He willingly died in our place and saved us from our sins. Without Him nothing is possible.

THE AUTHORS

Tim Chaffey is a husband, father, pastor, teacher, cancer survivor, author, and apologist, with a passion for reaching young people with the gospel. He earned a B.S. and M.A. in Biblical and Theological Studies, a Master of Divinity specializing in Apologetics and Theology, and a Th.M. in Church History and Theology.

Tim is the content manager for the Ark Encounter and Creation Museum. He is also the founder of Risen Ministries, which is home to his blog, podcast, and speaking ministry. He has written over a dozen books, including *The Remnant Trilogy* and *In Defense of Easter: Answering Critical Challenges to the Resurrection of Jesus.*

Joe Westbrook is a husband, father, occasional writer and blogger, aspiring theologian, and amateur woodworker. He pays the bills by working in a hospital lab, though he has ambitions to find a creative career that can be accomplished out of his home.

Joe lives in central Iowa. You can follow his exploits on Facebook by searching for Central Iowa Craftsman, Central Iowa Theologian, or Joe Westbrook Author.